THE ULYSSES PACT

KARTHIK C

REDGRAB books
redgrabbooks.com

Title : The Ulysses Pact
Author : Karthik C

Published By
Redgrab books Pvt. Ltd.
942, Mutthiganj, Prayagraj, 211003
www.redgrabbooks.com
contact@redgrabbooks.com

Printed and bound in Manipal Technologies Limited, Manipal, Karnataka
Paperback, First published by Redgrab Books Pvt. Ltd. in 2021
ISBN : 978-93-90944-40-8
Copyright © Karthik C 2021
Printing rights reserved : Redgrab Books Pvt. Ltd. 2021
Cover design and Typeset in Redgrab Books arts

₹

Dedication

All the words are magic,
Kindred spirits waiting to be dramatic;
Stories they tell are true.
Hope and despair:
Always go hand in hand,
Respite from them you will find;
Among these pages written for you.

Hidden in this acrostic with glee,
Dear, I write for thee!

ACKNOWLEDGEMENTS

They say that writing a book is an endeavor that no sane man undertakes. It is indeed a difficult process but I am glad that there are people around me who made it easier. Be it by their constant encouragement or their willingness to leave me alone. I am thankful for that and have to acknowledge my wife, parents, daughter and my pet. I am grateful for Redgrab books private limited for their support and cover designers for their work. I am indebted to all my friends and family from whom I have learnt a lot. Too all the people looking for second chances, persevere, and you will prosper.

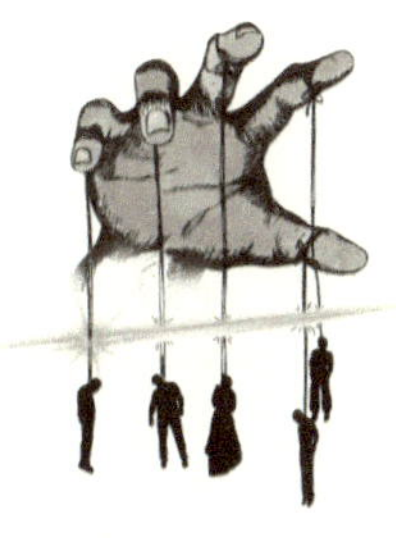

PREFACE

The story that you are about to read bears the name 'The Ulysses Pact' which is an ancient understanding elucidated in the 'Odyssey' by the great Homer. It is currently a part of behavioral psychology which broadly means 'to lock us in'. It is a freely made decision that is designed and intended to bind oneself in the future.

The same is true in this story of second chances, where the characters are made to be bound to their days of hope and not plunge themselves in to the deep abyss.

There have been innumerable peer reviewed articles on psychoanalysis which suggests that as everything is in this physical plane, pain too is relative. We as humans have undergone a tremendous fine tuning on an evolutionary scale where we imbibe everything thrown at us and adapt to it. To fast-track this, we need a frame of reference. The reference is relative to the subject perceiving it, if the subject is in pain and if the reference point is someone or something in a condition much worse than him/her, then their personal pain appears trivial. This coping mechanism is ingrained in our wires. There is a famous saying attributed to many, from Shakespeare to Mahatma, from Tolstoy to Saadi Shirazi which goes something like this: 'I cried because I had no shoes until I met a man who had no feet'. This is the essence of life.

Our age old mythology too has some parallels to support this claim, where a dejected Pandava Prince Yudhisthira is exiled after the fateful game of dice. He is consoled by the wise and virtuous Saint Dhoumya who regales the tales of the Kings of yore: Harishchandra, Nala and Nahusha who fell from grace. He asks the Prince to learn from their mistakes and get back up and importantly, when compared to them, the tribulations of the Pandavas were minuscule.

The story which follows is very close to my heart where the characters go through testing times but also shows that together, we can overcome any obstacles that comes our way. I hope you are enthralled by it and when you finish it, you are filled with positivity and optimism.

The pages that follow are written with passion and among those are tales of social drama, a murder mystery, a love story, international espionage, psychological suspense and an overarching thriller to keep you engaged. I have faith that you will enjoy reading it as much as I have enjoyed writing them.

Karthik C

CONTENTS

THE ULYSSES PACT

It had been years since the fall of Troy. Helen was back with Menelaus in Sparta. Agamemnon had razed the once glorious city to dust. The debris swallowing the blood and bones of heroes and lovers alike. The city was buried along with Achilles, Paris, Hector and Prium. A war fought on the basis of love, ended where finally none remained. Odysseus or Ulysses stood on his ship as he reminisced the war and the tribulations that he had to endure to reach Ithaca, to reach his home, to reach his love, to reach Penelope. He knew that it was not over yet.

He was very near the hollowed islands of Sirenumscopuli which was inhabited by the deadly Sirens. Legend had it that these Sirens would lure nearby sailors with their enchanting music and singing voices to shipwreck on the rocky coast of their island. Ulysses knew about the myth but the arrogance in him wanted to experience the singing. He ordered his men to apply beeswax to their ears so that they will be deaf to the music, and asked himself to be tied to the mast, so that he could not jump into the sea, entranced by their haunting voice. He ordered them not to change the course under any circumstances and to keep their swords upon him and to attack him if he should break free of his bonds. They were to overrule his future command on the contrary of what was stipulated now, regarding this matter. This pact would go on to save the life of Ulysses, as he was driven temporarily insane by the songs of the siren and commanded, attacked and pleaded with his men to cut him loose which would have certainly caused his death. The contract, which was a freely made decision that was designed and intended to bind oneself in the future would go on to save many lives from their forthcoming deaths. This was the Ulysses Pact.

***

CHAPTER 1

The metallic squeaking repeated itself regularly giving the cringe inducing noise a weird rhythm and flow. The glint of the steel was dim, as the dullness around appeared to smudge all the colors making the random shapes to overlay on each other with no differentiating features. The misshapen hands rolled the swaying wheels through the darkness and into the light where the murmurs were apprehensive. The noise died down as the creaks of the wheel rose. As the wheelchair moved ahead into the tunnel of light, the dullness evaporated, and the color spread into the room engulfing the bland silhouettes and replacing them with discernable shapes with defined contours.

The featureless morphed into radiant people sitting expectantly in a decorated room. The plastic chairs were draped in faux satin and a bright red tape was tied around it, knotting in the back forming a big bow. The Sunday morning sunlight pierced through the sealed glass windows which was installed high near the roof on all the walls. An expecting woman in her last trimester sat in the front row caressing her husband's hand on her bloated tummy. The husband was enjoying the little kicks from within and it looked like the woman had had one kick too many. A baby was crying in the middle as the grandmother was rocking it to and fro, while the mother rummaged through her pregnant bag to look for the bottle. A small girl dressed all in pink screamed and ran with a red balloon with a parent behind her tail. A college student was looking at his phone, oblivious to his surroundings. A newly married couple were talking to each other in hushed tones constructing their dreams together in the back. A father was jumping up and down to get to the red balloon which was now stuck near one of the sealed glass windows as the kid in pink cried beside.

There was a sexagenarian looking at his old HMT Janata watch. Every time he looked at the time, he was also looking at the memories. He caressed the long, black, wristband, remembering the time when he was relevant. Remembering the time when he was gifted this watch by his dying father as a token of his ascension as the 'man of the house'. It was so like his father, saying without saying that his time was up, and it was time for his son to step up. He had worn the watch through all the trials and tribulations that life had thrown at him. Each time he wanted to give up, he felt the weight of his watch, weight of his father's expectant glare coming beyond the grave; telling, asking, pleading him to move on. Just one more step. That's it. You are done. But he knew there would be another right after that. That's how you made me walk father. Each scratch and tear on the watch showed his fight and he wore it with pride, like a bragging right, a big old fuck-you to life. Who said time-machines didn't exist? But he was done. He wanted to close the loop now. He not just wanted to travel back in time and return, he wanted to stay there. Stay there with his father. Forever. Period.

He slowly rolled his wheelchair, entering into the hall and moving further down the narrow passage leading to the empty stage to which he had no desire of reaching. The darkness cleared in his eyes and he saw the people who were sitting on either side of him. The squeaking of his wheels had caused them to look at him. Some showed recognition and others stared in wonderment at the frail man sitting in the wheelchair, wearing a crisp white shirt and a navy-blue pant. He was wearing a gray, tweed, checkered flat cap which masked most of his forehead and the shadow from the stiff brim covered the rest of his visage.

"I died fifteen years ago. I died trying to save you ungrateful people by sacrificing my family," said the voice coming from the wheelchair. His lips didn't appear to move but it looked like the sound came from within him, from some buried and broken part of him. He stopped rolling and pulled the brake lever beside one of his wheels. The squeaking stopped but was quickly replaced by ticking. The ticking increased in sound and frequency and was drowned the next moment by a ball of fire which seemed to compete with the sun. All the glass windows were shattered, and the cars started to beep in the parking because of the explosion. The wheelchair was thrown near the distant wall, now crumpled as a searing steel football. The mangled bodies were strewn everywhere giving the appearance of an unholy anatomy, experimented by a deranged God. Two pretty bows were burning, forming a charred cross on the remaining parts of the chairs, they acted as unmarked tombstones for the mass grave that had formed in an instant. In the middle was a frail hand, completely stripped of skin but with a black analogue HMT Janata watch, in-tact, where the ticking continued, and the clock stuck 12.

CHAPTER 2

Yazdaan Abbas woke up to the increasing sound of the alarm going off on his phone which was next to a battered black wrist watch. He looked at the time and it was 12:00 AM. He took a gulp of water from the bottle kept on a table beside him and slowly walked to the bathroom and took a leak. The house was dark and there was a slow rumble in the sky outside. Yazdaan went from his small bedroom and into the guest room which acted as his home office too. He sat behind the desk and booted up his hibernating laptop. He unlocked the cabinet beside his desk and took out a huge manila folder along with five bulky red files with each marked from Subject A to E on a white tape. He spread the files on his table like playing cards and perused through them one after another. There were photos, case sheets, medical and psych records, hand written notes, news clippings and other sundry items. As he was looking through the last file, his laptop screen came alive with a video call, inviting him for a video conference. A bright red word started blinking. Abyss. It was time.

He made sure that his military grade VPN and double encryption protocols were working, and the anonymous call was coming through a TOR browser. He was in the Deep Web. He put on his headphones and accepted the call from the organization just called the Abyss. There were eight members logged in apart from him, the inner circle of the Abyss, and everyone except the moderator was on mute. The video screen was dark and slowly went a bit bright as a dim light switched on in the background. Yazdaan reflectively ran his thumb across the yellow Batman sticker which was pasted across the lens of his integrated webcam. Absolute anonymity was the name of the game. The moderator appeared with the faint light behind him which masked all his features giving him the appearance of a garish silhouette. It was also clear that, as usual, he was wearing a balaclava. He spoke first, and it was apparent that, like Yazdaan, he too, like everyone else in the call, was using voice masking software. His voice was not robotic but gave out a low-pitched effeminate tone.

"I believe Operation Overton Window is a go?" It was difficult to say if his English was broken or was done deliberately but even in his artificial tone there was a hint of authority, a stamp of ownership but above all an incorrigible enlightenment which went well with his username, The666Saint.

"It is. I was able to access the funds yesterday. A small delay as I had to reroute from the Cayman Islands through a third-party vendor mining in cryptocurrencies. Some traffic due to server breakdowns in the southern hemisphere. The location and technology and more importantly the *resources* are all in place. All systems are a go," said Yazdaan or Uly55e5PT, as his username went.

"How's the… er… publicity?" asked Rated9RDX, "that's what will ensure our return on investment."

"Care to update Tra5h9anda1?" asked The666Saint.

"All the right feelers are sent. Contacted all the usual suspects and a few new players... eager players. But, if we are to sustain, it depends on the presentation. It depends on the participation, on the pawns and last but not the least, the necessary outcome. After everything is said and done, this is essentially gambling and my clients..."

"Our clients...," corrected The666Saint immediately.

"Our clients," continued Tra5h9anda1, "expect odds and considering their rather substantial investments, favoring odds which we cannot provide given that this is a novel venture which has not been tried yet."

"This is the Dark Net Tra5h9anda1. We are also catering to fetishes which is our USP. They are our priority. The gamblers are only the surface. We can skim them out if the need arises," said Xca1ibur.

"The perverts can't sustain you. Remember, if what Uly55e5PT says is true, and practical, this will take months and may be years till a pawn is taken out of the game... or rather takes himself... or herself out of the game, till they see even a dollar of return. The perverts will lose interest by then. They will jump ship to catch some other new fad in the zeitgeist. It is the gamblers, the opportunists who will be the last men standing... or women."

"If I may pitch," said Uly55e5PT, "I agree Tra5h9anda1. This is an experimental venture involving people's psyche which at the very least is unstable, considering our guinea pigs, but given the location and the power that we hold, and their inherent and current vulnerability, utterly controllable.

For the sake of posterity, let me again shortly explain; maybe this will help in convincing that the perverts will be interested till the inevitable end and help in further promoting this.

What I have at the ready are five pawns in my game. Each carrying a rather heavy emotional baggage filled with regret, lost opportunities, failures and guilt, not to mention all of them have tried committing suicide at one point or another in their life. Me being a licensed psychiatrist, have recruited these patients into an experimental clinical trial where the alleged objective is to observe the alterations in emotional and physical wellbeing of a subject and betterment in their suicidal ideation through co-sharing and co-staying in a controlled environment with similar subjects. Let me assure you gentlemen, these subjects are at the very brink. I have already shared their case copies, their colorful history, albeit for obvious reasons, their names and addresses have been redacted. The initial interest was because of the history and believe you me, they will retell their own history, with their names to all our clients. The program is designed to get our desired results. This is our odds.

The location is custom designed to suit our needs. A Big-Brotheresque house catering to all their needs, all under the umbrella of surveillance with what them being prone to self-harm, an efficient way to monitor them. By using state of the art motion sensing HD cameras able to simulcast through our deep networks live, we will be able to capture every minute details and interactions of our pawns. I already have their informed consent on their agreement into the clinical trial, them being filmed, them being administered experimental drugs which are not yet approved by any of the federal drug agencies. I have some magical compounds which can help us nudge them in the right direction. They will be addressing me as Dr. Aman Abbas, which will be my nom de guerre.

Every minute detail is taken into consideration.

A one of a kind reality show catered to our different clients where there are no eliminations, the doors are always open, if the pawn feels, after sharing and staying with others that his will to survive increases, then he is free to leave. Contrary to most shows, the last contestant standing is the loser, quite literally, as he or she still is caught in the proverbial spider's web."

"Which, let me reiterate, we do not want to happen to only a single member," said BullTower69 for the first time.

"Yes, indeed. We need every one of them to lose. Loud and clear," agreed The666Saint.

"Agreed," said Yazdaan, "that will be our motive, with the chemicals and the activities, we will be seeing less and less of our contestants and not because they went out of the house, I hope you get the picture."

"All right. Thank you Uly55e5PT for that. I hope we all know clearly what our venture is. Put it simply, our pawns will be entering a house of death. Our opportunistic clients will be betting on which of the psychologically damaged contestant will try to kill themselves and if they do indeed try, then on whether they will survive. This itself will incentivize our misogynistic clients, fueling their perversity. We will double down on the feelers and the remaining agreed sum will be dispatched in the next hour. There are no servers up for maintenance today anywhere I believe, so you will face no delay there. I will share the portals to access the network as and when this goes live which, according to schedule will be no later than 0530 GMT tomorrow. Bear in mind that the portals are dynamic and will be auto-notified if there is a change. Also, just to refresh, for our opportunistic gamblers who will not be inclined to watch the stream 24/7, there will be a dedicated team of data scientists who will analyze, curate and present the data on real time basis based on their individual preferences and requirements so that they can make an informed decision while betting, obviously at an extra price. If there are no more questions, then we will again meet at our scheduled time. Depth to Abyss," said The666Saint as the connection was terminated.

Yazdaan shut his laptop down and wiped his brow. He knew the money would be there by tonight. There was no turning back now. The easy part was done. It was time for the big show.

CHAPTER 3

The sun was slowly setting down in the sky. The light late autumn breeze had a sting to it as the pollens were well on their way to complete their mission, their fate, their destiny. To prepare for the upcoming spring, to bring life. The five 'contestants' sat in the garden after returning from their mandated itinerary. A purple sunbird was chirping on the single lemon tree almost devoid of all its leaves, the only tree in the garden, singing good bye to the setting sun retiring for the night with a hope of a new start tomorrow. A new beginning.

"The day," said Avinash Naik looking at the lemon tree, "has been… eventful."

"Yes. I… er… yes. Indeed, it has," said Pierre Menard who slowly slid to the ground and cradled his knees.

"There is just no justice. My whole upbringing revolved around pleasing the almighty. To pray for his forgiveness. To atone for my sins. What a joke! There is no God. Not one. Not ever. If there is indeed a God, I would not want to pray to him. He is not supreme, he is depraved. Who will he atone his sins to? I mean… those were kids damn it. Toddlers who are just opening their eyes and they have to endure… this? Endure us? And those innocent stray animals! My heart just goes to them," said Dhruv Rao as he wiped his nose.

"I mean yes, the world is filled with filth and I do not want to sound selfish here. All of us here are depressed, though I do not know you all personally and your history, but we are all together in this study because of Dr. Aman. And let's face it, we are here to get better. I get this place. Away from the city, away from all the hustle, away from all our vices and technology. Nature's basket, playing, cooking, reading, and exercise and meditation. Yes, makes sense. But sending us to a place like that? That's brutal. How is that supposed to help us?" said Avinash.

"It has. I mean look at Dhruv. He may be talking about all the darkness, but he is also empathizing. He is caring for others. We have to go beyond that. As Aman keeps saying, we have to understand that there are others who are enduring far worse than us. They are dealt with a bad hand right at their birth. We need to trivialize our sufferings, though it will not be easy, to move forward, to swallow and stand up again," said Sharma.

"I guess you are right," said Pierre after a long silence, "I mean, this is the last straw right! No going back. It's all or nothing. Yes, we will get better. In retrospect, I would like to apologize to all of you for my behavior these couple of days. Dignity of labor and all that entitled shit that I tried to pull."

"Hey… No need for apologies here. This is a judgement free zone. These things are bound to happen when you put strangers together in a house," said Avinash, "I agree with Sharma too. Now I see the difference. I don't want to quantify each other's pain but rationally, now I have a frame of reference, a different perspective. I mean we worked with kids who were terminally ill, who are in coma, who were abused, orphans, who… who are autistic, who are at-risk. Volunteered at an animal shelter. How can you even be in your own cooped up cocoon when you see them fighting, surviving?"

"Don't forget what we did today either. I think that is the major takeaway today. When we went there, we forgot about our bickering, about our baggage and we worked together to bring a difference in their day. I can't wait to go back again tomorrow. We made them smile guys. Kudos to us. We made them happy. All of us… together," said Supriya Sinha holding Dhruv's hand and giving it a warm shake.

"True. Its almost been a week now. Let's make this day even more eventful. We are here to share right? Let's do that. Let's share. We have been too inhibited by our past, by the choices that we have made. We have to move past it," said Pierre, "As Avinash said and… as Dr. Aman keeps saying, this is a judgement free zone. We are in a controlled environment. I understand that we may react differently after getting to know who we really are but that's the risk we were willing to take. That's why we agreed to this trial. If you want, I will start tonight. I will be the ice-breaker. Do you want to listen to my story?"

Everyone looked at each other and slowly nodded to Pierre with varying degrees of a smile.

"We would be happy to," said Sharma, "thanks for taking the initiative. But let's have some ground rules. There may be some parts of the story which we may very well be… illicit but bear in mind that we have all paid for it and there will absolutely be no judgement or critiquing. We will have a short timeout to clear our biases and return and be nothing but wholesome. Agreed?"

"Agreed," said everyone in unison and looked towards Pierre Menard.

CHAPTER 4

A Sanskrit Subhashita of yore:

काकः कृष्णः पिकः कृष्णः को भेद पिककाकयोः
वसन्तसमये प्राप्ते काकः काकः पिकः पिकः

[Kakah krishna pikah krishna, Ko bheda pika kaka yoho?
Vasanta samaye praptey, Kakah kakah pikah pikaha]

The raven is black, and the cuckoo is black
What difference, then, between a raven and a cuckoo?
When spring arrives, it's easy to tell
That the raven is a raven, and the cuckoo a cuckoo.

Pierre Menard looked up from his laptop screen to catch a glimpse at the running ticker tape on his TV. The brightness on his screen was at a sharp contrast to his haggard visage. There was nothing bright or cheery on his face. The salt and pepper beard was anything but rugged on his frail countenance and the dark circles were gaining ground each passing day. There were days when girls found him attractive, beautiful even. The high cheekbones and the so-called ogee curve on his lips made him a decent figure to look at, but all that was drowned due to his indulgence of looking at a bright blank screen for most of his days and to sink his desperate sorrows by draining his drink. All perks of being a writer.

Pierre Menard had always wanted to be a writer. He had never had any other ambitions, not even when he was a child. He remembered him sitting alone at his beloved grand ma, his meesa's place, spending the joyous summers by reading stacks of books which he was too young to understand and write scrawny notes which made little sense to others. His teenage years were no different. Spending his time at his meesa's place, his friends playing football or volleyball at the hippie riddled shores of North Goa and he was on a shack reading Elmore Leonard or Le Carre' with a chilled beer.

He was not a person who would boast about his talents or intellect with others, but Pierre knew that he was a wretched person inside. He called it a curse, to be enlightened, as he always felt annoyed or irritated by others and the system at whole where he felt they were satisfied by leading a mechanical mediocre life. We were all programmed where the powers that be had convinced us that the benchmark for our existence was to become an engineer, work for a multinational by selling our soul and identity, earn and climb up the contemptable capitalistic ladder and marry according to your archaic customs and traditions and continue the broken and vulgar system. Where the hell was living?

He had understood a very long-time back that nihilism was his way of life and found extreme passion and joy by writing make believe stories. There was nothing interesting in the society and he was too timid and lazy to change it. The only way that he felt alive was when he infused life into his characters. The divine feeling of giving and taking life and controlling someone, albeit imaginary, gave him a profound sense of self-worth. He was contented in only that. He would chastise himself that his thoughts would populate the entire 'iamverysmart' subreddit, that's how self-aware he thought he was.

The 'news anchor' was screaming at something or someone and so were his esteemed and informed panelists. There was seizure inducing amount of information flashing on and off the screen and 'breaking news' covering half of it. Among the cacophony, he saw the ticker tape again, a small scroll saying simply that a famous novelist had unsuccessfully sued another for plagiarism.

"Fuck this," said Pierre.

"Pierre, language please," came the voice from the kitchen.

Instinctively, he looked at Mary who was busy playing with her lego bricks. She was so engrossed in the ship that she was supposedly building and failing miserably that he was sure that she had not heard his pejorative. Mary was his daughter, half conceived as an experiment and half to fulfil his rudimentary duty as a husband. He loved the little ball of dough with all his heart but if given a choice, he would trade her for a good book, no questions asked. He had realized that his was a lost cause, marriage and writing would never go hand in hand. It was a fool's pipe dream to expect a cozy living by writing alone. Sure, Pierre had had his master's degree and had found a 9 to 5 job as his vocation only to sustain himself with no urge of grandeur in it. He was happy if the bills were paid and he had a full stomach so that he can sit and bleed on the paper. That was exactly it, writing was just sitting and bleeding on the paper.

"How many times should I remind you to watch your mouth? At least when Mary's around," said Julie coming from the kitchen and blocking his view of the TV, as she arranged her and Mary's lunch boxes on the table.

Pierre went back to staring at his blank screen with a mock expression of disdain. Anyone, anyone who still believed in the custom of marriage that is, would be lucky to have Julie as their wife. She was well adjusted and educated, had a nice paying job and was absolutely beautiful. She was loving and caring and more importantly, rational. Pierre had met her first on one of his visits to his meesa's place in Goa. She had a nice catholic upbringing and maintained her chastity until Pierre had arrived. She was the prize of entire Colvale village. A bragging right, a trophy to be had for anyone who banged her, and Pierre had done just that. He had charmed her with poetic quotes and read her passages of Jane Austen while listening to moonlight sonata as the Arabian sea kissed their toes. As providence would have it, their correspondence continued in Bangalore where Julie was also working. He did not know that it was not luck, certainly not good luck, which had caused this. As he had expected, the trophy was his. She was a beast in the sack which made it hard for him to have a minimalistic approach to her. He kept craving more and the power of lust always trumped his ego until it was too late.

The great Pierre Menard had slipped, and the nice catholic upbringing meant that it would be a shotgun wedding and so he stood next to his pregnant wife with a fake smile plastered across his face. One summer at his meesa's place had changed his entire life. He was just a happy-go-lucky boy from Bangalore spending his long weekend from his milquetoast misanthropic life in the beaches of Goa and just like that he was married and expecting a child in a few months. He looked at his child as a guinea pig to see if he could discern any of his intelligence, if eugenics had played any part and in two and a half years, he had not seen any distinguishing features. He had published a few short stories in assorted magazines and some well received critical articles on the current affairs, but his novel had hit stagnancy long before he was married but he blamed the lack of progress on his wedding.

Listening to the forced sound of the packing of lunch boxes, Pierre sensed that an apology was in order.

"Sorry Julie, it won't happen again. I will put a tenner in the swear jar," said Pierre, "It is just that I saw a news scroll which said that a writer whom I know (he didn't), couldn't sue another writer after he had stolen his work. Blatant plagiarism, these fools do not understand what it takes to come up with an original idea and write it convincingly and entertainingly. Only a writer can be Jack of all trades and master of all too."

"What are you talking about?" said Julie. She doesn't understand. No surprise there. You feminists claim mansplaining is wrong, but you never do understand on your own.

"Let me explain," said Pierre, "I will take an example of Angels and Demons. You have read it."

"Which one is it again?" said Julie as she picked Mary and made her sit on the sofa as she looked for her shoes.

"Jesus Christ," said Pierre exasperatingly, though he did not believe in the magical messiah, "The one with the Illuminati, the one with all the ambigrams," said Pierre and when he saw that it was of no help, "the one with the symbols where words can be read both upright and upside down, which you thought was a good idea for tattoos." How original!

"Oh yes, that. Right… right… and please don't take our Lord's name in vain," said Julie buckling Mary's shoes, "Go on."

He let that one go. He was in no mood to go on that tangent. Religion was a circus. Having imaginary friends was fine till a certain age. "The author, Dan Brown, has to have Master's level knowledge on geography, Papal order, Vatican city, history of that place, science and technology behind antimatter to write the story but telling all of it to a layman who doesn't understand any of these, all the while moving the plot and not boring the idiot sitting on the toilet and reading this is where the real art lies."

"Hmmm, yes. I understand. Stealing is never OK. They are breaking a commandment," said Julie as she hurriedly carried Mary and her bags and rushed towards the door, "catch you later, bye."

Hmmm. What is that? Hmmm. It is not even a word. This is what you get when you think with your dick instead of your brain. This is what started most of the fights. He would prick her time and again on how she had ruined his life, that he could never fulfil his dreams of being an accomplished author. His life would just be like everyone else's. Just another brick in the wall. He had manipulated her in forcing her to take a job right after Mary's birth without giving her the time to recuperate. Gaslighting and guilt trip were one hell of a weapon. His retorts on each and everything had irritated her and urged her to get out of the house more. The materialist in him was happy at the idea. He quit his job and became a full-time writer in its truest sense. Julie was the bread winner, she did all the work, paid the bills, did the household chores, cooking, taking care of Mary and Pierre. Pierre knew that Julie did not know that he was emotionally raping her, that she was the victim and that brought him a weird sense of accomplishment and joy, a victimless crime he called it. Her body had lost its allure, more so with Mary's birth. She was just another part in the cog wheels running the assembly line for a capitalistic corporate. He was sapiosexual, intelligence attracted him, aroused him and he craved intellectual women to fulfil his libido.

Frustrated, he got up with breadcrumbs falling from his chest, from the huge ergonomic chair which Julie had brought him begrudgingly after hinting many times, though not subtly, that the couch was affecting his productivity. He walked towards the door with his bath robe dragging across the floor, like a cape of an out of shape, out of work, middle aged superhero. He closed the main door shut. He looked forward to this activity every day, closing the door on reality. His quantum of solace.

* * *

Pierre Menard sat down to write. He adjusted the height and back support of his chair, decreased the brightness of his screen, arranged the pen and his trustworthy diary full of his innovative ideas on the table. He called her Helen, his muse. He had jotted down all of his epiphanies, his repository for all his future books. He took a sip of water from the bottle and rubbed his hands together and kept his fingers gingerly on the keys. The attention to detail mattered, everything had to be just right, his own sacred ritual. He was sure that he was going to run through his thoughts and spit it out at enormous speed. He was afraid that he may ruin the keypad of his laptop with all the typing.

"Don't be absurd," Pierre chided himself smiling. Even he knew the extent of his exaggeration and the limits to it. Slowly, the smile rescinded, and an expressionless face looked at the blinking pointer on the blank screen as if chiding him, daring him to catch it. How much ever he wrote, the blinking pointer would be one letter ahead of him, always.

"Please, oh non-existent God, let today not be like yesterday," said Pierre aloud and typed some gibberish in utter frustration. The meaningless drivel filled him up with even more rage causing him to hammer down on the backspace key. He got up and spread the yoga mat in the center of the living room. Maybe meditation was what he needed. He closed his eyes and took a deep breath and held it in and exhaled completely and stopped, playing with his mortality as the blood drained from his brain. He probably had too many brain cells which might have been the root cause of all his troubles. As his mind wandered on its own existence, Pierre got up, giving up after relentless absurd thoughts bombarded him with lightning speed.

"Why can't the plot flow through me like this? Is there a malevolent puppet-master taking ecstasy at the cost of my tribulations?"

He dug through the fridge to get himself some jam for a simple toast after rejecting everything that Julie had cooked for him, maybe the hour since he last ate his breakfast was too much time, he needed refueling.

"That's one way to lose your appetite," said Pierre after first trying to watch a YouTube video on how to make French toast resulting him in wasting an hour and a half through its rabbit hole ultimately ending in home birthing videos. "What the hell did I just watch?" said Pierre before ordering out. Pierre continued to look for the spark needed for him to write by playing fortnite and spewing expletives at teenage strangers, listening to Chopin, reading in the toilet, dozing off on the table, playing with the lego bricks and just browsing through social media until he heard his wife and kid coming through the atrium. The day was done. He hurriedly sat at his desk, wearing his horn-rimmed glasses and crumpling some paper from a notepad and throwing it purposefully to miss the basket.

"Hi papa," said Mary as she came running to Pierre who hugged her by bending down and kissed her on the cheeks.

"How was school, sweetheart?" asked Pierre.

"Chaya miss taught us three rhymes," said Mary holding two fingers.

"Oh, how nice. Tell them to papa when I come in to tuck you in angel," said Pierre wondering whether his hopes on Mary being like him was in vain after her finger show.

"Will you not ask how my day was sweetheart?" said Julie as she kissed him on his cheek.

"How was your day honey?" asked Pierre playing the part of the husband. It was like he was on a play which was repeating every day and he himself was an audience. A weird Groundhog Day type of situation.

"It was horrible. My manager took credit for the Ruth and sons account, the one which I told you about, completely, right in front of my team. The smug bastard had the audacity to look me in the eye and smirk. I am fed up of this. Asshole ruined my entire quarter and gave me a pounding migraine," said Julie as she dropped her bags and went to the kitchen, "give me an hour and dinner will be served.

"I am so sorry dear," Pierre feigned. He did not remember who Ruth and sons were and he couldn't care less. If you are in the wild, sheep were bound to be eaten by wolves.

"Mary," screamed Julie as there was loud noise of utensils dropping to the floor, "look at what you did, you spilled all the milk. Go to your room and stay there until I ask you to come. Your ice-cream can wait till tomorrow."

Pierre strained his neck from above the screen and looked at Julie standing beside the fridge, completely defeated.

"Want any help baby?" said Pierre.

"Want any help? I am completely drained from work and I have to prepare dinner, wash the dishes, need to check on Mary's school work, fold the hanging clothes, iron the uniform and feed her and get her to bed, and sit and complete my job for which I do not get credit and do not get paid enough and before all this, I need to clean the mess and go out and bring milk for our child and you ask if any help is needed. So, to answer your question, NO. Thanks. You please sit and concentrate on your writing because God-forbid if you get up from the chair and do something else, Armageddon may be upon us. It is blasphemous to even think of such a thing. It is like there is a ticking bomb attached to your seat which will detonate if you get up. Just like everything else in this house, I will manage," said Julie as she took the purse and stormed out of the house.

Pierre looked at her with a sullen face and got up with a forlorn look. He saw Mary peeping through the curtains of her room and smiled at her. He went to the kitchen and got the mop and started cleaning the flood of milk.

"People need to learn to mind their own business. The aunty downstairs asked if you were a paraplegic. But in a sense, they are right, you are a recluse," said Julie as she barged in with packets of milk and a loaf of bread and seeing Pierre in the kitchen, "Oh, please your highness, go back to your throne, we peasants will do the chores."

"That's it," said Pierre, "quit nagging. If you cannot deal with the responsibilities, then quit that too and accept how you ruined my life. I will go get a job tomorrow itself. I cannot deal with this crap day in and day out. You think I lead a contented life by sitting at home every day and you are the only one who toils? Sit and come up with anything creative and then I will accept your criticism. Just when I was in the zone you do this every damn time. Fuck this." It is he who stormed out of the house now.

* * *

Pierre Menard sat at his usual table in his usual pub sipping his usual drink. Good old Mr. Monk. Nothing beats a good rum with coke. He never was a big drinker. He was a teetotaler until he upgraded himself to a social drinker, just because that's what writers do, but now the drink drains smoothly and quickly with no curfew on it not being a social occasion.

"This city is doomed. We are doomed," said Vasanth as he slapped the shoulder of Pierre as an acknowledgement of his arrival and sat down heavily on the tall chair opposite him. Vasanth and Pierre had been friends from their school days and had been haunting the same pub ever since they started drinking, although at different times. Vasanth prided himself on his well-kept body; a budding fitness freak, gym filled the void his wife had left when she divorced him. It's a harsh irony that fitness would have indeed saved his marriage in the first place.

"And what is it this time?" said Pierre as he motioned for one more drink for his guest to the waiter.

"Traffic. You know that the distance is measured in time now! How did we get to this? And don't give me 'you are traffic' crap. I am here to lose steam so please allow me to do just that."

Pierre smiled and lifted his hands feigning his surrender, "Go ahead, I am here to do the same."

"Dwight was right. We do need a new plague, that small nosed asshole," said Vasanth loosening his tie.

"Hey, come on now, don't start on The Office. I will not be able to hold it in."

"That's what she said."

"Holy shit. I fell right into it."

"That's what…."

"Shut up," said Pierre as both laughed and high-fived.

"So… what's bothering you? Wife and kid, I bet."

"Don't trivialize things. You know me. It is always me. I am the problem. It is my writing. Writers are good at two things. Number one. Procrastinating when there are solid ideas. Number two. Getting stuck with writer's block when there is an actual urge to write. And as I am a writer, I am good at both. The bottom line is, I am not doing what a writer should essentially be doing, writing."

"Let me guess, this is straining the family string which is already taut. I understand. No, really, I do. And you know what? I might actually be of some help to you this time. Good that you brought this up. It had completely slipped my mind."

"I highly doubt you do. Offence intended," said Pierre as he emptied his glass and motioned for a refill. "Have you ever written anything creative? You are just patronizing me by saying you understand. Your empathy is actually insulting my friend."

"You are an asshole when sober but man, you turn into a flaming pile of dog turd when drunk. But before I forget or change my mind because of your warm attitude, the latter is much more likely, there is a writer's retreat which is happening in Sakleshpur."

"Oh…, tell me more."

"I will, now shut up. We had gone to a homestay-resort in Sakleshpur called Manju over the weekend. 'Mandatory company outing'. It was supposed to increase morality to achieve the unrealistic targets set to us. Anyway, sales is my bitch to take care. When we were leaving, I saw the registration book. They are hosting a weeklong writer's retreat starting next month. It is sponsored by some of the prominent publishing houses. Hidden valley creative workshop for writers, if my memory serves," said Vasanth as he meddled with his phone. "Here, I have shared the contact info of the resort. You can go online and check if reservation is needed from the organizer's website. Food, lodging and workshops among likeminded people amidst nature's cradle. I bet that is what you need. To just get away from the routine. You have been cooped up in that little nest of yours for far too long. Get out, breathe some fresh air, talk to people. Talk to like- minded people. Share and discuss but for all that's holy, get the hell out."

"Hidden valley creative workshop," said Pierre thinking as he checked the number shared by Vasanth and he quickly googled the event and read through the itinerary, organizers and panelists, "they have a good presence in social media. Maybe it's time for me to lift my ban on them. This might just be what I am looking for. Change might be all that I need. Thank you."

"There is nothing social about you and don't thank me yet. It's as if I was meant to be here with a panacea to all your maladies. Here, you ass wipe. Now, go. Get lost. Go and fuck your beautiful wife for me," said Vasanth as he slipped a small plastic packet which he had taken out from his shirt pocket across the table under his palm.

"What's this?" said Pierre slowly checking his surroundings before peering into the opaque Ziploc packet.

"A new nootropic drug my sponsor wants us to push. I tell you, we marketing folks in pharmaceuticals are just glorified drug peddlers. The doctors prescribe medicine to their patients not based on the drug's safety and efficacy but based on the number of international trips the pharma companies are willing to sponsor. Fuck health and fuck ethics and we are at the forefront of it. We are pimps collecting money from our customers to fuck our own whores. How crazy is that! Let that sink in. Anyway, this is the new it drug in the market. Untested. Unlicensed. Unapproved. Under clinical trial. But some of my physician friends tell me that it is safe, and they try it regularly. Makes their hectic life a lot easier. Cognitive enhancers. Brainchild of precision medicine, a limitless super smart drug. Take one when you really want to write."

"Fuck you. You think I need chemical assistance to herald my creativity? You are insulting my intelligence. My brain is my drug."

"Cool. If you don't want it then flush it down the toilet. Being a zonal manager has some perks," said Vasanth tapping the shirt pocket. "All I ask is to keep it with you. Never say never. At least have it till the workshop is over."

"All right. I will have to convince Julie on the retreat and also to fund it. The workshop is not cheap," said Pierre tapping the screen of his phone where the registration page for the retreat was now open.

"I know it will not be a problem for a manipulative monster like you."

"No problem at all," said Pierre as they raised their glasses to the thought of taking advantage of a helpless woman.

* * *

"Yes, you are right, in a sense that writers tend to go in a fugue state, a sort of forced hibernation, allowing thoughts to percolate through the filters of their subconscious and slowly allowing their random thoughts and ideas to coalesce into a coherent plot," said Pierre, "But to what end? We need to have a trick to fool our boastful mind, a tripwire, a trigger effect if you will to set a chain reaction, to unlock or destroy the withstanding threshold. To… to break the dam per se."

"I understand the frustration. If you are a writer, doesn't matter if you are prolific or not, you have to accept the dreaded block. No other way around it. But one thing which comes to my mind, which helps me, is what the great Hunter S. Thomson used to do," said Johnathan Myers, the New York Times bestselling author, "We all know the crazy genius, the pioneer of gonzo journalism and all his 'in the face' type of writing. But when he was starting, in his college days, he used a weird technique just to get into the mindset of a writer. He used to reproduce, word for word, a novel which was already written. Just sit and write a published novel, which he had read, from start to finish. He famously reproduced The Great Gatsby like this. It was like F. Scott Fitzgerald would possess you and allow you to write. What he used to do was a menial, mundane activity but subconsciously, he was preparing his mind to explore the author thoroughly and tuning his body by allowing it to adjust and adapt to the physical toll of sitting at the same place for extended periods of time. Maybe this, as you so rightly said, tricks our brain to unlock the threshold. But again, it is a subjective technique. But writing something than nothing helps to keep the frustration out which is the first hurdle to be productive."

"Yes. Thanks a lot Johnathan and thanks to all our other panelists. Unfortunately, that's all the time we have folks. To sum it up, as they say, there are only three rules for writing. 1. Read a lot. 2. Write a lot. And lastly and most importantly 3. There are no rules for writing. I hope you have enjoyed the workshop as I know you have enjoyed the scenery. It has been very interactive and informative. We have learnt a lot from each other and hope that we go back and inculcate all we have imbibed here and finally throw up on those insulting white blank pages. Enjoy the rest of your stay and happy writing everybody," said the organizer ending the last scheduled event.

The three-day workshop had been spaced well to unwind and relax. The resort was right in the middle of the mighty western Ghats where green covered, sun kissed hills stood sentry all around. The peaks were eternally engulfed by the clouds as if the Gods had taken offence at their unholy heights and had robbed them of their achievement. The birds were chirping, and the trees were rustling as the gentle breeze swayed time and time again, taking away the stress and strain by every passing minute. The 'no network – TV free' zone was like a time capsule with clock running behind and minds running ahead. The silence had been unsettling to Pierre at first but had slowly grown fond of the calming effect it brought with it. With all the events done, Pierre got himself a stiff drink (rum and coke, what else?) and sat beside the bonfire, gazing at the starlit night sky.

"How long has it been since you saw a clear sky like that?" said a woman approaching him.

"Long," said Pierre looking at the woman. She was slim but busty at all the right places and had freckles creating the shape of the bat on her face which made her look young. She had so obviously dyed her hair red to go with the freckles, thought Pierre, embracing the Irish way and was actually pulling it off, thanks to the lack of melanin and probably hemoglobin too.

"I enjoyed your excerpt yesterday. I look forward to reading more from you. Don't forget me when you get famous. By the way, this is the last night for us to put off writing. Tomorrow we go to war," said the woman, "I am Priya. Priya Kamath."

"Yup it is. Thanks. Hi Priya. I am Pierre," said Pierre shaking his hand which lasted for a bit long than it probably should have.

"That's why I am not wasting it being sober. Some try by making their body a vessel for dead writers to possess and I am experimenting with this," said Priya looking at the golden-brown scotch glinting from the fire.

"Hey, you are not alone," said Pierre raising his glass as they downed their liquids and laughed, "How about one more?"

"This is already my forth. Why stop there? Let's go, I have a bottle of rum and whiskey in my room which I don't intend to take back home" said Priya as she slowly blinked and smiled at Pierre. Pierre got up and helped Priya to her feet slowly and walked hand in hand laughing at this and that as they entered Priya's room and closed the door behind.

* * *

The blank screen was not blank anymore. Pierre could feel the blood pounding in his brain. It was as if the brain decided that it needed all the fuel available to keep the churning on at full speed. Everything else around him was a blur. He could only subconsciously discern various shapes of his wife and kid come in and go in his periphery as he focused every bit of his creativity on writing. He made spurious notes, researched fervently, read voraciously and wrote like there was no tomorrow. He ate less and slept even less and was not able to tell the time of the day as dawn and dusk appeared to fuse with each other. He had never felt like this before. The gears had shifted, he was actually in the zone. He finally felt alive.

The retreat had indeed helped. Julie was sane enough not to hamper his rhythm. Yes, he was now what he wanted to be, a writer who cared little about anything else other than just write. For fifteen long days and equally long nights Pierre wrote and, in that fortnight, he was able to come up with an idea, research on it, conceptualize, create suitable characters, sew a coherent plot, complete a draft and then edit and polish it with utmost care and submit the finalized manuscript to his publisher. His first child, Pierre thought. But what about Mary? No... Mary belonged not just to him. And besides, he never wanted to have her anyway. But this... this was his and his alone and a creation of not just passionate want, but a lifelong penance stemmed from fervent need. My baby. My precious.

* * *

Prabhu S. Chawla had been a banker for most of his adult life. He had gone the way of the expected. Get into a B school (through donation from his businessman father) and settle into the world of numbers and manipulation. He had never dreamed of leaving his niche world and become a writer. He did not dream to be one nor was he passionate about it. But he was good at telling lies and once on a decadent pub crawl with his friends, he told how easy it is to manipulate a market if you are in a position of power or if you were well endowed with vitamin M, and when one of his friend had told that this would not be possible in the field of writing and publishing, Prabhu S. Chawla on a whim, fueled by his desire to prove his friend wrong had taken to writing.

He struggled to piece a sentence at first but as time went on, he was caught by the writing bug and was able to complete a short book, a pulp fiction, catering to the lowest common denominator. The language was dry and vulgar with no hint of finesse in it and the characters were bland and one dimensional, but it had all the ingredients of a pot boiler. Drugs, sex and violence. As he had calculated, there was a trend of bankers turned authors ruling the market and with his power of authority through money, he was able to find a respectable publisher. The (paid) editor had to work day in day out to make the novella half decent for public consumption and as luck would have it, it became an instant bestseller, thanks to the overall decline of IQ in the society as a whole. This led to further book deals, a sequel, another standalone novel, a collaborative novel with an American bestseller, film deal with a reputed studio and a wagon load of endorsements.

Prabhu S. Chawla soon became an ex-banker and a prolific writer frequently attending panels in literature festivals, a social media influencer and was also somehow perceived as a political commentator for reasons yet unknown. Everything was as he had envisaged. You just need that one novel to establish you, the brand did the rest. You can coast on that name till the day you died which Prabhu intended to. So, it came as a shock to him when he heard that his publisher was dropping him as their client after the debacle with his latest novel. The critics and the users had panned his book as utter drivel. Some critic had called it a string of non-sequiturs which dared the readers to move on. If the writer was wondering when he would be ousted for his terrible writing, then this would be it. But Prabhu S. Chawla was not worried, he believed in the established order of catering to the one who were once successful even if they were not presently worthy. Historical data defines future outcomes, for better or for the worse. But there always was that one iota of uncertainty, in any given field, which would slap you right in the face with their sudden righteous enlightenment and that was what happened exactly. Not a man used to failures or a modest human to learn from it, Prabhu S. Chawla strode into the publishing house.

"You drop me through a text?" said Prabhu S. Chawla sitting down on the chair opposite to the editor-in-chief of Peregrine Publishing.

"What? I had asked my secretary to convey this hard decision through the right channels. It was supposed to reach you through an official mail sent to your assistant, copied to you, of course. This is unforgivable," said Irfan Khader. He had no intentions of doing this.

It was not his first rodeo.

"Cut the crap Irfan, don't be sly. You know who you are talking to," said Prabhu S. Chawla shifting in his seat, "and besides, that is not the point. After all that I have done to your iceberg hit publishing house, the millions that you made out of my books, this is how you treat me? I am not one of your whores, the wannabe authors that you seduce and ward off like dung beetles after your one-night stands."

"Now, come on. No need to get personal. As a banker, you know very well that it was just business. I had to drop you. I had to think of the company, overseas market and board pressure and all that shit."

"You are not serious, are you?"

"I am afraid I am. I am sorry to tell you; your books will doom us all. The fuel of your reputation can only carry you, carry us, till here."

"Doom you? If you think that book was so bad, why the hell did you go ahead and publish it?"

"It was an error in our decision. It is all on me. There was no proper oversight and that problem is internal and is already taken care of. But I can assure you that it will not repeat."

"My God… look at your tone, one bad book and you are out, is that it?"

"Oh, how the turn tables," said Irfan with a smile.

"You think this is a joke?" said Prabhu S. Chawla getting up from his chair, flustered, "You are throwing Office references now?

I can sue you, you know that right?"

"We are well within our rights. You know it and stop shouting. That's all you were ever good at, your books screamed too," said Irfan reclining back smugly. The gloves were off now.

"You are nothing without me. I know your clients, who do you think can replace me? You think anyone in there has what it takes to replace Prabhu S. Chawla?" said Prabhu S. Chawla pointing to the pile of manuscripts lying on the corner of the table and pushing them down. The manuscripts fell and covered the large desk, pushing Irfan's laptop almost out of it.

"Forget about these," said Irfan pushing back his laptop in frustration, "I could throw a stone at a random person on the street and get a better writer than you. I think our business here is done."

"Oh, is that so? Then these here must be from Dickens and Dostoevsky. Let me see the intellectually stimulating fictional fantasy world created by the prodigies over here," said Prabhu S. Chawla as he picked one of the manuscripts lying on the table and skimmed through the pages before looking at the title page, "A Raven's Dream by Pierre Menard. Hmmm. Future Prabhu S. Chawla right here."

"That's enough. You have no right to read the works of my prospective clients," said Irfan but Prabhu S. Chawla had gone suddenly silent. He stood motionless reading through the first page of the manuscript in his hand. "What happened? Are you all right?" Irfan sat straight, obviously concerned about his visitor.

"What is this? What the fuck is this?" said Prabhu S. Chawla as he started to flip through the pages of the manuscript, stopping here and there to read some portions of it and stabbing it with his fat fingers, "What are you trying to pull off here? You drop me as your client and want to publish my own work again under a different name?"

"What absolute bollocks! Are you completely out of your mind? Go home and seek some medical attention. I do not have time for this nonsense."

"You think I am kidding? Look for yourself," said Prabhu S. Chawla as he slammed the manuscript on the table and turned it to face Irfan, "this is my work. You ripped my work and trying to publish it under this… this Pierre Menard's name. This is my novel. The Cuckoo's life. My most bestselling book. Same exact copy. Carbon. Same characters, plot, phrases, sentences, words. Word for word."

Now it was Irfan who got up from his chair. "Why will I try to publish a copy of a book already published by me? To what end? Let me have a look," said Irfan as he wore his spectacles and stretched his arm out.

"You were well within your right, but not anymore my friend," said Prabhu S. Chawla, handing the manuscript to Irfan.

"Look, this is still a manuscript. This is not a book. It is not official. Do you see my publishing logo anywhere on this? If you have to sue anyone then sue the writer who was audacious enough or more likely, stupid enough to steal so vehemently and steal a mediocre book at that."

"I will not rest until the score is settled with you. As the name suggests, you are a bird of prey. Feast on our carrion you vulture. I need the name and contact details of this cretin."

Peregrine means falcon you moron. "Ask Mandira on your way out, she will provide you with it. Do whatever you please with it and don't mind coming back. Security will not be welcoming," said Irfan as he watched Prabhu S. Chawla storm out of his room, and he slammed the manuscript hard on his desk before he sighed and slumped back on his chair and called for the editorial assistant who had put the manuscript on his desk.

"How could this have happened?" said Irfan comparing the paperback novel and the manuscript, holding The Cuckoo's Life in his left and The Raven's Dream on his right hand.

"I am sorry sir. I am new here and I had not read The Cuckoo's Life before today," said Nethra, the editorial assistant.

"You might have not read but this Pierre Menard has certainly read it. This is blatant plagiarism. Fuck him. I hope he has the same audaciousness to deal with Prabhu S. Chawla's wrath. With all his power and money, along with the misery of him losing us as his publisher, he would drown this Pierre guy. No doubt about it."

* * *

Pierre Menard stood in the small wooden stand at the district sessions court. He was the defendant with a criminal case accusing him of blatant plagiarism with an additional charge of defamation where he was sued for five hundred crores for slandering the intellectual property of the rightful author. He had noted all the ideas since their inception in his trusted notepad, Helen. Was it possible that Helen had invited trojan viruses which corrupted his system? No, Helen would never betray him.

The prosecutor was reading from a pile of papers cluttered on a desk filled with documents. The defense lawyer who Pierre had found based on his asking rate and not on his ratings and reputation was doing what was expected, resting on his palm waiting for the trial to end with no signs of interest to defend his client. The judge was looking at his phone as he nodded intermittently. Prabhu S. Chawla seemed like the only person who was paying any attention. There was a sense of smugness and also a hint of contentment written on his face, not because he was winning, which he certainly was, but it was as if he was finding a weird form of sexual relief from all of this. It was as though everyone present here were part of his debauched carnal fantasy.

Pierre just stood there, staring. Staring at the pile of files strewn across the judge's table. The pages had already yellowed, cases buried in time, justice forgotten. He stared at the still half-done paint job on the opposite wall. The line of people with dejected and defeated eyes waiting for their turn, waiting for the impartial land of law to prevail and take them out of their misery and into the mystical and mythical place of light where everyone was equal, and all was fair. He stared at the black mold in the corner creeping ever so high in defiance to the fresh paint on the other side. The darkness of corruption and rotten system sneaking in and glowing, blinding us all like it had the Lady Justice.

As Pierre stood in the defendant stand with his spatial memory in ruins, being comfortably numb, there were many who came and went in the prosecution stand. Prabhu S. Chawla, the organizer of the writer's retreat, Irfan Khader, the editor-in-chief of Peregrine Publishing, Nethra, its editorial assistant, and some who were irrelevant to the case but testified nonetheless. But he looked up to the stand when Priya, his companion from the retreat came and stood in the stand.

"I had not met Pierre before. But, yes, it's true that we spent the night together," said Priya as she answered the question of the prosecutor which Pierre had not heard. Pierre blinked twice and turned his face instinctively towards the people sitting in the courtroom. He saw Julie wiping away her tears as she carried Mary and walked out of the hall. He knew it was the last straw. He would not see his wife and kid ever again outside a courthouse. It was over.

"I can also attest that what he is telling here is lies. Pierre had indeed read The Cuckoo's Life. I know for a fact because I was carrying that book with me during the retreat. It was in my bag the night he spent with me in my room. The next morning, the book was on the table near the coffee machine, away from my bag. He must have taken it out after I slept off. Now, I am not saying that he read the entire book that night, but he very well knows that the book exists." She looked him dead in the eyes filled with revulsion before stepping down from the stand.

Pierre realized that this was the final nail in the coffin. That was it. His high hopes of everything that he intended to be was shattered. It was as if he could literally feel the physical pain as his life-long dream was torn and taken away from him.

"Let's get on with it then. Finally, does the defendant has anything to say?" said the judge as he turned and looked at Pierre with his half-closed accusative eyes filled with saturated numbness.

"I… I do not, your honor, have anything to say in my defense, except that I understand," said Pierre adjusting his faltering voice and looking up at the judge, he would not be ashamed, he would keep his head held high, he had done nothing wrong though pretty soon he would be judged and convicted for it, "but I would like to share something with everyone if the court permits."

And without waiting, he continued, "I was ousted before the charges were filed, before I received a summons for the trial, before there was a complaint, or a lawsuit notice against me. I was berated in the media, be it social, print or visual, when the case was still subjudice. Innocent until proven guilty? What a joke! But I understand. I really do understand. When you understand stuff, the inner machinations of the universe and how futile our existence is, and to know that life has no meaning, Solipsism kicks in and you have to force meaning into your being to spend your designated time in this curved reality, otherwise it will become physically hard to even breathe. The perks of enlightenment."

"Now to do that, all you have is to create your own world, have your own characters and make them interact the way you would want the world around you to be. To achieve divinity by creating stuff. This… this was what I was good at. I knew only this in my horrid life. Fantasy was my drug, my catharsis. I would trade my organs for a good book, trade my non-existent soul to the non-existent devil for a good review on my work. And I thought I was good at it. I thought I was one of the few who would make a reader forget his misery, where he could immerse himself in my work, forgetting his troubles, laughing and crying with my characters, follow, dream, enjoy and empathize with them. Be entertained, enthralled. Now all that has changed. But still, I understand."

"My passion has become my poison. A writer is like a virus. They can only be alive if there is a suitable host. If there are no readers, then writers will be extinct. This… has made sure that no one ever will read any of my work. Even if I reproduce the finest literature mankind has conjured, it will be orphaned because of the plagiarism tag. The label of a thief is branded on my forehead which can never be erased. But it has erased my lust, my love, my life. I understand this too."

"You know what the cruel irony of it all is? I know that my wife and kid will leave me because of what happened here today. In some corner of my depraved heart, I actually wished for it. This was how much I loved writing. Because of the curse of enlightenment, I knew that writing had to be a solitary journey, because of the monetary and meditative aspects of it. You must be a saint. Now, my wish is answered but the payment for its fulfilment is sacrificing my writing. The miserable irony, the ultimate killing joke. The bottom line is that you must pay the piper. I am left with shattered dreams and a broken family. Even though I know I have not consciously wronged, I understand that the evidence points to the contrary. I have lost, pure and simple. I have lost everything, even myself, by not knowing what happened. By not knowing how it happened. This is what is killing me from within. This is what is tearing me apart from inside. I understand everything, but I could not understand myself. This… I do not understand."

"Yes… all right. For us to understand and to come to a decision, we need testimonies and attestations. The court works on proofs and it is quite clear that you are guilty and as the court has seen and analyzed your finances, I can only pass the proof of judgement on the defamation case, you cannot get blood from a stone, I hope this is fine with the prosecutor," the prosecution nodded their approval as the judge continued, taking the gavel in his hand, ready to strike down his judgement, "Fine, and on the criminal proceeding of the copyright infringement and plagiarism, I find you, Pierre Menard, on this count to be guilty under IPC section 378 and proclaim a punishment of six months of imprisonment open to probation after three and fifty thousand rupees in fine for the court. The session is adjourned." The mallet of justice had once again faltered.

* * *

Pierre Menard stumbled down from the bed laughing. The red shimmering liquid spilled on the ice-cold floor of the room. Priya too was laughing uncontrollably as she was trying to drain out what little drops that were left in her last remaining scotch. Pierre slowly got up and sat on the edge of the bed and kept his empty glass on the table next to the coffee machine. This was new for Pierre. This was uncharted territory, his to claim. He found himself attracted towards Priya. She was licking the last drops from the glass laughing manically as he took the glass away from her.

"There's nothing there, come now," said Pierre trying to steady her.

"You owe me a glass of drink," said Priya pointing to the spilled liquor on the floor as her laughter seized and her eyes were getting dazed.

"I promise to get you two tomorrow," said Pierre holding her face in his palms and slowly sliding it to the nape. It was now or never. Seize the day.

And just as he moved for the kiss her head fell on his shoulder and Pierre knew that she was out cold. His mind wandered in the twilight zone where he contemplated the ethics of informed consent and if it would be him taking advantage if he went ahead and fucked her. But he restrained himself as he made her lie on the pillow and covered her with the sheets. Pierre sighed but also felt enthusiastic for the next few days. He had felt the retreat to be useful. He was sure that his writing would improve, and the wordcount would increase and as an afterthought, he remembered the smart drug. Yes, an added incentive never hurt anyone. He opened the Ziploc bag and took out the vial with the single drug inside a plastic pustule. There was a small package insert which he read hurriedly.

This modified version of Piracetam, the so-called smart/super drug, binds to alpha-amino-3-hydroxy-5-methyl-4-isoxazolepropionic acid (AMPA) receptor causing fluidity of neuronal membranes resulting in enhanced cognition. It has a very short half-life for a better PK and PD. The most common side effect is, ironically, memory loss, selective or otherwise.

He laughed at the humor in it and popped the small white tablet into his mouth and walked briskly to the drawer near the bed and took a gulp of water from the bottle. He saw Priya's bag lying open on the drawer and could see a worn-out copy of a novel jutting out of it. Instinctively, he picked it up and turned it around, reading the blurb and author's section and in under a minute, he was well into the book, sitting by the table with the coffee machine and turning the pages with great zeal as the drug and alcohol turned inside him with great zest.

Within an hour he had completed the book and stretched his arms. What absolute drivel! thought Pierre. It's my time to write. I will dethrone you Mr. Prabhu S. Chawla. I will rid the society of this garbage. But first, he needed a smoke. There was a pack in his car. He got up from the chair and walked out of the room and into the wilderness. The crickets were chirping, and few embers were fizzling here and there from the bonfires. The area was completely deserted, and the chillness of the night was rising. Pierre walked across the small patch of the shrubbery to reach his room on the other side of the homestay. He heard a small rustle near the road leading to the nearby village which ran through the gates of the resort. Pierre walked towards the sound in abject determination fueled by blind chemical induced courage.

"Take that bag, come on, move it. Fast," said one silhouette to another.

"Hold that wire, here. Let me get through this, I think that's a laptop bag right there," said the third.

"What are you doing? You are breaking into the cars of the guests," said Pierre.

The three men looked at each other and then at Pierre and then the one closest to him hit him in the head with the long metallic torch that he was carrying. Pierre swayed once and crashed on the floor instantly.

Pierre woke up after a while and looked around in the dark. He was confused of his surrounding and then realized that he was standing next to his car. He remembered that he had come to his car to get cigarettes. Too much of alcohol had caused a black out, he thought. He opened the door and took the pack and lit one and walked back into his room as he rubbed the small bump on his head caused because of his fall as an idea for a new book started forming in his head, which he would note down in Helen, blissfully unaware that he had taken a nootropic drug, had read The Cuckoos's Life and had been attacked which resulted in him being a victim of crypto-amnesia which would ruin his world.

CHAPTER 5

"I didn't know I would love knitting so much," said Sharma, "and stitching. That was really cathartic." The five sat together in the living room overlooking the garden and sipping their favorite juice and beverages.

"I know right! We are too quick to dismiss certain activities due to the flawed social construct built around it. We, especially men, either think that some activities are juvenile or effeminate. We are the losers here. We couldn't relish the creative release because of those activities which are perceived 'off-limits' to us. But no more. I have found my hobby. It is origami and ikebana for me. Who knew folding paper and arranging flower would fill up my void?" said Pierre marveling at the folded butterfly in his hands.

"It is still a surprise to me that woodworking is my calling. Sculpting something beautiful out of a dead log, infusing life into a lifeless thing to avoid rot. That's some philosophy right there," said Avinash.

"I am even more happy and proud that we were able to learn these arts and crafts this past week from people who are differently abled, acid attack victims and rape survivors," said Supriya, "they make me want to be a better painter and maybe that will help in bringing some color back to my life."

"I am sure it will," said Dhruv.

"What about you Dhruv? Did you find something that you want to explore?" asked Avinash.

"Pottery. You just need the right guiding hands to mold and make something useful from mush, to make something hard which can hold and withstand the troubles life throws at you. To get acceptance," said Dhruv.

"If it's all right with you all. I would like your time tonight. better to get this over with. Yes?" said Avinash.

"Yes," said everyone smiling.

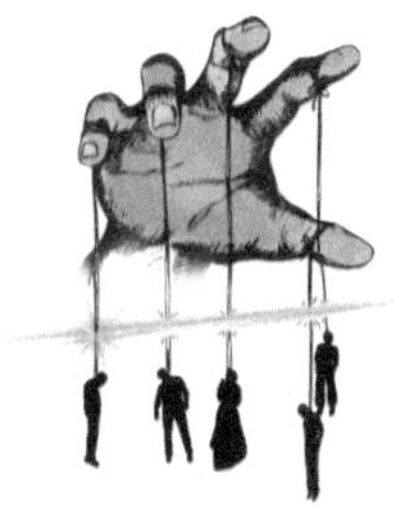

CHAPTER 6

Heavy unseasonal rain battered against the windshield. High winds made it even harder to drive on the dark new moon night. The highway leading into the city of Mysore was slippery which made it difficult to control the gyrating car even though it was being driven slowly. The air conditioner had stopped working, making Avinash Naik to lean ahead and wipe the foggy glass in front of him. He was trembling behind the wheels and was completely disoriented. He had to squint hard to see the myriad curves on the dark road. The street lights were off too, adding to his misery.

He drove at a snail's pace until there was some respite from the rain. Seeing a lonely uninhabited alleyway on the side of the road, he pulled his sedan to the deserted curb and got out. He took a couple of nervous steps from his running vehicle and looked around, trying to be sure that no one else was there and walked deep into the cul-de-sac. With a shivering finger, he unzipped his pants and started to relieve himself on the end of the curb. He saw a shadow move behind him and instinctively turned around to look at a stranger in front of him. This night would test him to his limits. He was surprised by that thought registering to him at such a dangerous moment. The man was as tall as Avi and was heavily built. The rain started again and battered his face. The sudden lightning gave Avi a chance to have a look at this stranger. He was young with dark features and he had a silver ring pierced on his left eyebrow which sparkled.

"Hand over your wallet," said the stranger.

Not now, not today. "Leave me alone or I will call the police," said Avi trying to intimidate.

The stranger quietly and expertly took a wooden club out of his shirt collar which was expertly hid in his back and said nothing.

"Just… relax… and you can have my wallet," said Avi, slowly inserting his hand inside his pocket to retrieve his wallet. There was a loud thunder and acting on some primal instinct, Avi pounced on his threat hoping that he was distracted by the devastating sound. The stranger agilely stepped aside and averted the attack. He swung his log with all his might, and it hit its mark. Avi had ringing in his ears and he lost his balance and collapsed on the wet ground. He felt something warm flowing on his cheeks and massive hands probing him. Then everything went even more darker.

* * *

Avi struggled to open his heavy eyes. Someone was calling his name. He wanted to scream at them, pleading them to stop. There was something more important that he wanted to tell, which was fast slipping off. He woke up with a blinding pain across his temple.

Getting up was not an option. Thankfully, he dozed off and woke up after what felt like an eternity.

"You were found by a garbage pickup truck in a lonely street yesterday morning. They brought you bleeding from the head. We have sutured the lacerated scalp. Luckily, there are no internal clots. It seems that you had suffered a blow to your head just above your right ear by what seems to be a blunt instrument. All reports are normal, and your condition is stable. But as you were unconscious, there might be a slight concussion. You will be kept under observation today," said the doctor in a very soothing voice, "we called your office by the number we got from your identity card. Couple of your colleagues are waiting outside. We couldn't find any other belongings of yours. No wallet and no cell phone. We found a movie ticket stub for day before yesterday's evening show in your pocket and nothing else. Do you remember what happened?" A police constable was standing next to him with a notebook.

As Avi tried to remember, a blinding pain shot through his temples. He waited for it to subside and then started, "I remember checking in at Jayamahal hotel at two and coming out of my room at four P.M. and must have gone to the new pirate's movie."

"Must have gone?" asked the constable.

"I don't remember it that well. No…, I had gone," replied Avi.

"How was the movie?" inquired the doctor.

"The movie was good. I had already seen it once. Just wanted to pass the time as my meeting was cancelled and I had nothing else to do. I… don't remember what happened after the movie."

"Don't worry Mr. Naik; you will be dazed for some days. These things are common in head injuries, blunt force trauma. The alleyway you were found is near to your hotel. I assume you were returning from the movie when you were attacked and robbed," concluded the doctor.

Avi just nodded his approval and the constable assured him that the culprit would be caught and left.

Two of Avi's colleagues came and wished him well. They informed him that they had taken the office documents which were recovered from his car. He listened to them and nodded absentmindedly. Only one thing was bothering him after all this. He didn't care about his injury or the robbery. All that he worried about was his wife, Anjali.

* * *

A few days earlier he had found out that Anjali was having an affair and that too with his close friend. He wanted to confront her. He had even thought of divorcing her. But now he wanted her more than ever.

They had been married for five years and had known each other since seven. They both had no one except themselves. They both had lost their parents when they were young, had no relatives and very few mutual friends. He had thought that their love was pure but was heartbroken when he saw her and his long-time friend entering a hotel room together. He was smart enough in inquiring about them at the reception without rising suspicion. His life spiraled down and collapsed when they confirmed that they were frequent visitors with a designated room. He had thought of never forgiving her but now he needed her. Maybe they needed to just sit down and talk. Coming this close to death, he realized how valuable she was. He was ready to forgive and forget. He would do anything to get things back to normal. He could convince her to stop seeing his friend. He had to make things work.

After all, she was the love of his life.

* * *

The next day, Avi dialed the number to his home and tried Anjali's cell phone. Repeatedly. But no response. Concerned, he collected his discharge form and next week's appointment for his follow-up and went to his car. He drove to Bangalore, all the while stopping and trying his wife's number at phone booths to no avail. He reached his house fast and went through the gate. Milk cartons and newspapers were lying on the compound untouched. He knocked on the door thrice. No response. He pounded on it out of sheer frustration. The door gave way and opened slightly. Hesitantly, he opened it completely and went inside calling his wife's name who was never this negligent. He walked past the hall and lost his balance. He saw his wife lying motionless on a pool of blood on the other side of the hall. The stench of the body was filling up the air. He collapsed on the floor sitting next to his beloved wife. His stomach was in knots and his tongue was dry and rubbery. He got to his feet and called the police. Within an hour, his house was swarming with strangers.

"The victim, Mrs. Anjali was hit in the head and seems to have died instantly. No valuables were stolen, so the murderer must be someone familiar. You were in Mysore for the last three days and you too were hit in the head and robbed. Spent the last two days in hospital. Returned back today and found your wife dead," the senior detective Murthy noted. The scrutinizing summary was cut short by the phone ringing. Avi answered the phone and it was Deepak. His close friend, the guy with whom Anjali was having an affair. He had called out of concern as he had not heard from Avi for a couple of days. A lot of emotions were running through his mind, so he just told him what had happened and cut the call.

Deepak came to his home as soon as possible. He stayed until the body was taken away for autopsy and the police and reporters had left. Only then did he try to console Avi.

"I know about you and Anjali. Our friendship died the day you slept with her. Please, get out," said Avi. He suspected Deepak to somehow be involved in this. He didn't want to jump into any conclusions. But he sensed it. Deepak just stood there for some time and left. His lack of response proved their affair. Avi was filled with hatred, anger and grief.

It was pitch dark. She was standing alone, her face was down, then something threw her away. She screamed and vanished.

"Anjali," Avi woke up with a start. The nightmare was vivid but made no sense. He spent the rest of the night thinking about the phantasmagoria.

* * *

"Your alibi checks out. You were in Mysore. The hotel camera has picked you leaving the lobby. And you left to watch a movie and the ticket issuer has seen you at the theatre where you had a fight with him regarding spare change," detective Murthy was telling over the phone to Avi. I had a fight at the theatre? Avi couldn't remember any of it. "The autopsy report says that your wife died on Thursday, late at night because of brain hemorrhage. I am terribly sorry. I can only envisage what it must be to lose a pregnant wife," said Murthy with a toneless voice.

She was pregnant? Why is it getting this hard? The whole world was spinning out of control and only Avi stood still. She was pregnant!

"And we have a breakthrough into the case too. We have found a set of fingerprints other than yours or Anjali's in your house. We are running it in our databases," Murthy was continuing.

"I know to whom those prints belong to. I know who killed my wife" said Avi and explained to Murthy about the affair his wife and friend were having. Murthy assured that he will follow the lead immediately.

"I did not kill her. She was telling that Avinash might already be aware of our affair and that she loved me and not him. She wanted to leave him and come with me. I refused. I wanted to get out of the relationship. I felt bad for Avi. I had made a mistake," said Deepak when he was brought in for questioning after his fingerprints matched with the prints found at Avi' s house, "I did not want to continue making the same mistake. It had to end. So, I went to her place after Avi left for Mysore. We had an argument about this topic. She was not ready to listen. I just pushed her away and stormed out of the house, closing the door after me, that's all."

"There is blood which was recovered from the edge of the TV table. You pushed Anjali and she lost balance, hitting her head on the table which caused her death. We are arresting you on the charges of involuntary man slaughter" said Murthy and took Deepak into custody.

* * *

A dark shadow was pacing along the floor followed by a razor-sharp motion of its arms. A woman screamed and then a loud thud was heard.

"Anjali," Avi yelled, trying to catch his breath. The nightmares didn't stop. Every night the same visions with minor changes. He still couldn't believe that his wife was dead, and his best friend was the reason for it. The only closure he could find was that justice was done.

"Deepak was granted bail and the charges were dropped because of lack of any substantial evidence," said Inspector Murthy the next afternoon.

"You are telling me that the person who was having an affair with my wife, the person who himself confessed pushing her to her death, while she was carrying my child, walks free?" said Avi.

"I am sorry, we can't prove anything right now. There is no intent to kill. Have patience and justice will be served" consoled Murthy and took leave leaving an incredulous Avi to himself.

* * *

The dark shadow loomed at the crying woman. There was a sharp swing of its extended hands. The woman was thrown out of her feet, screaming and crashing down.

"Anjali" Avi woke up, regaining his composure. He let out a shrieking sound. Deepak. Only one thing mattered to him now. Vengeance.

The day was beginning to break. His earphones were plugged in as he jogged. Kemmangundi was a pleasant change after all the commotion related to Anjali's death. The nice calm weather had a much-needed soothing effect on his mind and body. He ran from the dormitory to the top of the hill just before sunrise. The darkness of the night was slowly being engulfed by the piercing rays of the nascent sun. Shadows started to form. Deepak was trying to catch his breath near the end of the precipice. A long shadow was cast on him. Deepak turned and was face to face with a familiar figure.

Before he could react, he was pushed by Avi. He lost his balance and lunged forward about to plummet into the never-ending drop when Avi caught him by his leg and said, "All I did was just push" and then he let go of the leg. The sound of Deepak's screams decreased by the second as gravity did its merciless job. Then the screaming stopped abruptly. Closure. Justice in its own way, was served.

* * *

The dark shadow was breathing hard. The woman just stood there crying. It was raining outside. The shadow turned away from the woman, took something shiny and swung it across, again coming back to face the woman. The object hit its mark and the woman was thrown out of the ground and collapsed on the edge of the TV table, hitting her head on the same spot as the shiny thing had. She fell to the floor and remained motionless. There was lightning, and, in that instant, the dark shadow had a face. At that instant, Avi saw his own reflection on the black powerless screen of the TV.

"Anjali" Avi screamed; his clothes soaked in sweat. These weren't the same recurring nightmares. These were his repressed memory breaking out. Now he remembered. Everything. His heart wanted to break out of his chest. He tried to make sense of the revelation.

He had come to know about the affair. But he had to leave for Mysore for a meeting. After checking into the hotel at Mysore, he came to know that the meeting was cancelled. He went to the theatre to catch the Pirate's movie again. Had an altercation at the counter about his change because of his bad mood. After around ten minutes into the movie, he came out, not able to sit with the range of emotions running through him. Took his car out and made his journey back to Bangalore. After four hours, he reached home. He knocked, and Anjali opened the door. She went into the hall and started polishing a tall brass oil lamp, explaining that she had bought it the same day.

"You are home early. Meeting got cancelled?" said Anjali rubbing the new lamp vigorously.

"Yes. I… I know about you and Deepak" said Avi, hoping to get it over with.

She stopped rubbing it and stood. She wanted to say something, but the words never came, only tears did.

"I just saw Deepak's car leaving this very lane when I entered. Why Anjali?" said Avi pacing all along the hall.

"It didn't mean anything. It was just physical and nothing else" said Anjali. It was hard to comprehend what she was saying with all the sobbing, but he had heard enough. In a fit of rage, he took the brass lamp and swung it right across her forehead, causing her to rotate and fall back. On the way down, she hit her head on the TV table and collapsed on the ground. He knew the moment she touched the floor that she was dead.

Not knowing what to do, he left the house with the brass lamp still in his hand. He went to his car, getting drenched in the rain which had started abruptly. The lamp was washed clean by the rain. He opened a polythene cover from his car. Kept the lamp inside the cover and placed it on the front seat beside him and drove back towards Mysore. He drove through the night in rain and found a dark alleyway where he could dispose the lamp. He got out to check if he was indeed alone and that resulted in him being hit. As providence would have it, the lamp was one among the things that were robbed, the murder weapon.

"I killed my wife. I killed my unborn child. I killed my best friend. Justice must be done. I will confess and surrender. But I need to do one thing first. Absolute closure."

It was a new moon night. Heavy rains flooded the streets. The man with the silver ring on his eyebrow entered a deserted lane and stopped at a dumpster and started to relieve himself when suddenly out of nowhere a dark shadow moved behind him. He turned. Thud. Then everything went blank.

CHAPTER 7

"… and farming? Really? We can somehow understand pushing them to endure the emotional rollercoaster in helping the delinquents. But," said Rated9RDX.

"They are not delinquents. They were impoverished people, little kids and others who have suffered a lot," said Tra5h9anda1.

"Am I hearing right? Tra5h9anda1 is trying to be pedantic and fastidious with my wordings? You all realize that this may well hit us in our face, right?" said Rated9RDX.

"Let's get down to brass tacks," said The666Saint, "let me make it abundantly clear. The only way we are sustaining our audience is because they want to hear the rest of their stories. That's it. And to be frank, these side quests are not hurting them, it is hurting us. We do not want them to get better. Period."

"Agreed. No discussions there. Believe me when I say this that these activities are tailored to push them further down into the rabbit hole. We are burying them," said Uly55e5PT, "Their time spent with at-risk, terminally ill, handicapped and abuse victims will expediate their depression even more. Their recent week spent in the fields toiling with the poorest debt-ridden farmers and daily wage workers at the brink of death will act as a catalyst which will nudge them in the right direction."

"But their discussions after these activities seem to indicate the contrary. The only thing holding the viewers is their stories. If we run out of them, we are screwed.," said Rated9RDX.

"Give them time. Let these activities run its course. Their future is bleak, believe me. And besides, none of them have left the house, right?" said Uly55e5PT.

"All right," said The666Saint after a long pause, "We need to cut short. There is a small agricultural distress discussion going on now at the stream by our Five and we seem to have a new storyteller tonight. I think it will be the introverted weirdo Dhruv today. Let's meet again at our scheduled slot and hope for the better."

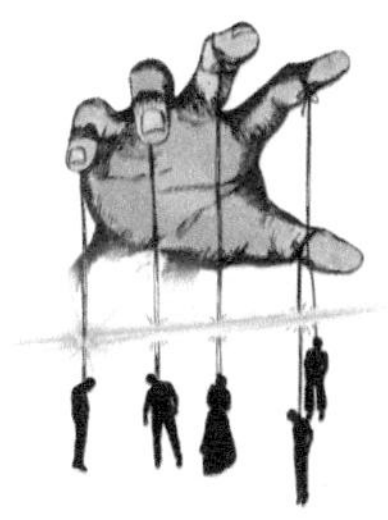

CHAPTER 8

All, everything that I understand,
I understand only because I love.
-Leo Tolstoy

There is something special about petrichor. For me, it was a gentle foreshadowing of pleasant things to come. The rhythmic battering of unseasonal rains against the carriage window formed myriad apophenic shapes on the glass, largely pareidolic in nature. The train trudged along its fixed serpentine track across the valley of mountains.

A kid, surprisingly bored by the breathtaking panorama outside became more indulgent, much to her parent's irritation, in running with the stuffed monkey which was held closed to her chest. The uninhibited love showed by the angel didn't fail to ooze life into the inanimate object as they danced together in pure compassion. The highly addictive charm and effervescent smile of a child was always an elixir to me as I sat and relished the beauty of nature both inside and outside my railway cabin. The innocence and naivety that they projected was a retrospective reminder of days gone by. A bitter/sweet nostalgia of what has been and what could have been.

* * *

I remember my childhood days in the picturesque village of Kigga in southwestern Karnataka right in the heart of the mighty Western Ghats. Being born into an orthodox, ultra-conservative Brahmin family was not easy. I was named Dhruv, Dhruv Rao; the brightest star albeit most of my life was engulfed in perpetual eclipse. Being a priest's son, I was forced to get up at the break of dawn during the cold mornings and take a shower from the icy water. I had to run to the village well shivering and get five buckets of water to the temple without spilling while climbing the steep stone steps bare foot. I had to bathe the main idol at the sanctum sanctorum in the temple of Nagareshwara, the Lord of the City. God Shiva in his traditional lingam form.

I didn't consider myself to be effeminate, but the rotund waist, the chubby cheeks, a more than pronounced symptom of gynecomastia and a single elongated tuft of hair tied in a knot on a tonsured head and the delicate, wet, transparent dothi never failed to embarrass me and make me a target for irreparable ridicule. It was a scene taken directly from Satyam Shivam Sundaram sans Zeenat's sensuousness and confidence among other things. She had Shashi Kapoor ogling at her and I had my ravenous peers ragging me.

I was always high from the smoke of the various havans being performed at the temple and the ever present khus-khus kheer. I hated every bit of my routine milquetoast lifestyle. You had to get up on your right side, eat, write, drink and start any other work with your right hand and you have to consciously enter any threshold with your right leg, be it a temple or a toilet which was highly unnatural and utterly difficult for someone who was a born south paw, which in itself was considered equivalent to breaking all the commandments.

The working of my family was a running manual for a wannabe OCD patient. The final brandishing was the sacred thread hung across my shoulder which confirmed my life long membership to the elite white cross society. It was an engineering marvel; a scratching device for my back though it was the reason for the itch in the first place and a secure key chain for my rusty Atlas cycle. It made its presence felt as it never failed to slide out of my half sleeves at the most inopportune moments especially in front of the physical trainer who had a personal vendetta against all Brahmins, and I was the scapegoat who had to endure his caste biased racial slurs for parading my creed.

I was a studious first bencher always first to class and the last to leave. I took tuitions in the evening to many tiny tots. A bookworm, seen always with a bag overflowing with dusty old books, after all bag was the signature of a student. An inviting site for last benchers to harass as they posed with their one book twirling on their forefinger.

The only quantum of solace that I could find was in the temple. Everyone was one as devotees; be it rich or poor, healthy or ill, young or old, man or woman. Though everyone was selfish in their prayers, they were a collective proof of humility, an acceptance that there is a greater power, a mighty force which aligned us all. I saw God in those pure eyes with their soul completely surrendered and I served him by serving them. By doing so I also earned an iota of respect and reverence. This was my purgation. Then everything changed.

* * *

It was my favorite time of the year. A celebration of the purest and unparalleled relation of a mother and her son. The festival of Gowri and Ganesha. They say we usually imbibe the characters of our favorite God. I unfortunately had taken the shape of my favorite one. I loved every bit of Ganesha, his intelligence, his round belly, his broken tusk and not to forget his elongated trunk and his vehicle of choice, a bandicoot. The festival spirit had engulfed the whole city. We had strived hard and collected funds from every nook and corner of our small locality to organize the puja, a tradition still followed from the pre-independence days started by Balgangadhar Tilak, to unite the nation against the rule of the British.

The seven-foot idol was in place at the corner of the road under the huge awning covering the entire lane. The rest of the road was to be covered by stage made up of small, square, wooden tables on which a renowned orchestra troop was supposed to perform the next day.

I was helping Girisha in arranging the stage. He used to live at the end of my street, and I used to call him anna, my elder brother. He used to give me wrist bands and bald tennis balls. I always looked up to him. He asked me to get down under the stage and tie the legs of the square tables to one another so that they wouldn't give way when they were stood upon. I obliged and started tying them together. I was bent on my knees, squeezing myself in the confined space and that's when I felt him behind me. Girisha was holding me. He started to touch and squeeze me. Before I could react, he was on me, kissing and licking. He was like a man possessed, groping and probing me as his nails and teeth bore into my tender skin. The shock had numbed my senses. I was in a catatonic state, panic commanding me into submission. I was frozen in hell right at the doorstep of heaven. That's when I saw him. My guardian angel, my savior.

Through the slit on the stage two twinkling eyes peered at me. There was something inherently positive that beamed from the endless, non-judgmental stare. Instead of calling for help I hid my face in complete shame, shutting my eyes as exhaustion seeped in. The next moment, the weight was off of me. When I opened my eyes, I saw a distorted silhouette fast retreating. A long slender arm stretched towards me. I was a bit circumspect and then reached out and held on to it gingerly. It was like a long-lost last piece of a huge jigsaw puzzle finally falling into place. The touch invigorated me and filled me with vigor. I tightened my grip and taking the cue the figure above pulled me up from the depth of darkness.

The red face with the twinkling eyes took me to his home and nursed the bite marks on my neck. I had come to the conclusion of ending it all once and for all. I would run away from here and would steal the large spool of plaited jute rope from our store room and tie a huge boulder to one end and the other to my feet and drown myself in the well.

But there was something about that face, something about the touch, something about this boy. The sharp nose above the enormous protruding lips and the large eyes gave him a smart but pallid appearance. He was unconventionally attractive and unintentionally warm towards me. His voice was soothing and his stare reassuring. The idea of me drowning drowned into the abyss of my brain and I felt drawn to this complete stranger who had saved me from the clutches of evil. He was the first person who had shown some care and interest towards me. My heart skipped a beat when he offered his hand and asked me to be his friend. I readily accepted masking the joy, for the fear of freaking him out, with great difficulty. His heart was synonymous with his name. It was indeed enormous, it was Vishal Kumar. This day had gone from becoming a bitter repressed memory to an unforgettable and memorable one. A whole new chapter had started in my non-existent life instead of ending abruptly. I was in the verge of losing my soul but instead had gained another. Vishal, my friend.

* * *

The next few years were the most joyous of my life. Vishal was the talk of the town. He was new to Kigga, recently shifted from Bangalore because of his dad's transfer. He was a city boy from a well to do family. He had all the latest gadgets and gizmos. From fancy cycle and digital watch to white sneakers and denim vests. Vishal being the center of attraction was obvious and I being his chosen friend was obviously not. My identity had changed completely. I metamorphosed from being the village dork to becoming the trusted sycophantic side kick of the charming teenage maverick.

I felt proud to be his only best and close friend. It was difficult to keep it that way. Vishal was sweet; he attracted a lot of ants. He had to be mine. Only mine, always. There were many threats but none so grave than Dhyaan Pai, our mutual plus one classmate. Vishal and Dhyaan were good in cricket, I was not. Vishal and Dhyaan were tall and fit, I was not. Vishal and Dhyaan were in NCC, I was not. He was nice to me, but I knew it was all an act to get close to my Vishal. I hated Dhyaan. I had to keep Vishal a safe distance away from Dhyaan. First, it was the small things. I had placed Vishal's cap in Dhyaan's backpack. I then enlightened Vishal on this little discrepancy by pointing a not so insinuating finger at Dhyaan and making sure that there was no confrontation between the two. I wanted the animosity to grow and also for the obvious reason of me not getting caught. The pattern continued. Vishal's bottle opener cum key chain, his sunglasses and other myriad knickknacks magically disappeared and then reappeared under the possession of Dhyaan. The coup de grace was when Vishal found his priced watch, a gift from his sweet grand ma lying inconspicuously in between Dhyaan's books. Dhyaan being poor didn't serve his case. Vishal didn't even acknowledge his existence from then on, let alone hear his side of the tale. Dhyaan was out of the picture. Peace prevailed.

I had not even uttered a single lie till then but had resorted to stealing to save my friendship and dare I say, my love. Yes, love. The feeling was more than liking, more than caring, more than friendship. It was love, the strongest of all human bonds. Yadbhavam tadbhavathi. What we feel is what we become. It was an inexpressible feeling of unhindered, saturated bliss and fulfillment. A perfect match. He was sagacious and loquacious, and I was laconic and taciturn. He was brave and beautiful, and I was brainy and bland. He was yin to my yang. We were destined to be together. Made for each other. I was not proud of what I did but the end justified the means. Besides, Dhyaan had to go. He was bad news. He was too, for the lack of a better word, possessive and I was just protective.

* * *

We had just completed our studies. Vishal barely completing and I in flying colors. That's when disaster struck. Without any sign or symptom Vishal's father passed away. It was a sudden and devastating blow. He was a good and caring man, always present to cater the needs of his only son. Vishal's mother had died giving birth to him, but such was his father's love towards him that he never felt the loss. The sight of an orphaned child is poignant and all the more so when it was my Vishal. Even after many months, he was still coming to terms to fill the void that his sweet father had left with anything but grief. I made sure that he never felt alone.

I remember the day when he was sobbing next to his father's grave with a bottle of beer in hand. There was heavy downpour all through the week. River Nalini was dangerously close to flooding. I had gone in search of him across the river, away from the village mainland only to find him sitting next to the grave. There were many other assorted beverage bottles. I knew he was in a completely inebriated state, a vulnerable man looking to drown his sorrow in alcohol. I scolded him and pulled him towards the bridge to get back home. He reluctantly followed hugging the bottles close to his chest. The temperature was unbelievably cold and both of us were drenched in icy cold shower and that's when the river bank broke and Nalini flowed uncontrollably, devouring everything in her path. The muddy bridge was no match to the mighty river. Suddenly it was dark all around. We both scampered in the moonless night and reached the abandoned shed at the end of the grave on a small incline filled with shrubbery.

We both drank the remaining bottles to keep ourselves warm from the monstrous climate. My first tryst with alcohol. The acrid taste of alcohol was like acid down my throat, but the warmth was soothing. It numbed my senses as we slept on the cold floor coiled against each other. And then instinctively, I kissed him. I don't know whether it was the alcohol or the compressed passion finding a release, but the kissing continued, and it was mutual. A chill ran through my spine as he hugged me and pulled me closer. At that moment I knew that it was the omnipotent love which was guiding us through. Love, the purveyor of heaven on earth. And I was in heaven that night. We writhed, twisted and turned and finally collapsed on to each other with me sleeping peacefully. Yes, he was in love too!

We never spoke about that glorious night again until the day Vishal announced that he was leaving to Bangalore to start a chit fund business with his uncle. My whole world started to collapse. He just mentioned the night as a passing joke, that he was straighter than a scale and that night was just a weird survival technique. I didn't push the matter any further as I had the other pressing topic of my love going away from me, though his words bit into my very soul. I was straight too. I was very certain of it. I never felt the least bit of attraction towards other boys. Never had the inclination to observe others too. I was attracted to him, only him. The idiot didn't get it. Gender and sex had nothing to do with it. As I saw him in the bus going away from me, I felt a part of me disappear. I had made up my mind. I was going to ditch the 'family business' and go to Bangalore soon. Go to Vishal, because heaven knows he needed me. Only one thing stopped me from doing it. My mother.

* * *

I had walked home keeping one dejected step after another. Everything had seemed surreal. I had willed myself not to lose hope. This was just a small hurdle. We will soon be together again. With that thought I quickened my pace and walked with a new-found purpose. I entered my house to what seemed a pretty usual scene. My mother was back from the hospital for the hundredth time. No doctor could diagnose what was wrong with her let alone treat her. All the usual suspects were present; my uncle, his enormously fat wife with her scaring make up and their blushing daughter, Lata. My mother had booked Lata to be my bride the day she had born and Lata, being the imbecile that she was had believed every bit of it. She was an unbearable nuisance.

But there was something different that day. The setting was serious and the tone hostile. Even Lata seemed to follow the decorum. Then my mother explained her recent visit to the doctor and told me that she had very less chance of recovering from God knows what and therefore very little time to live. All she wanted was to see her only son getting married to her brother's daughter. Her last wish as she put it. The news in itself was earth shattering. That's when I saw my mother as everyone else saw. She was frail and weak. Gone were the charming and radiant face which filled me up with warmth and the sharp, sparkling eyes were dry and almost vacant.

I obliged, not because I was being emotionally blackmailed, not because of the fear of losing my one true strength; but because I was confused. Vishal had left me. He had so blatantly abandoned me without even acknowledging or validating our love. Maybe it wasn't love after all. I thought I was stooping to blasphemy as it was sacrilegious to even think like that, but I conceded and within a week I was married at the temple. I didn't even inform Vishal, I knew not why.

* * *

Marriage was just a formality. I never even touched Lata. She was incredibly nice to me. Maybe she really did like me. Then unexpectedly, just like everything else in my life, I received a call from Vishal. Tears rushed to my eyes without any reason the moment I heard his voice. It was trouble. The chit fund business that he was involved had gone sour. He was deep in loan and the investors were volatile. Vishal was stuck between a rock and a hard place. His uncle had ditched him, and his partner had eloped with huge chunks of someone else's hard-earned money. He was depressed, desperate and alone. He needed me. I knew I had to act. I couldn't let my love die. Not after all that we had been through. Only large sums of money could save my friend and by extension my love too.

The street was deserted. At that time of the night even the holiest temple looked scary. I knew that the temple housed lots of cash and precious jewels. I just had to break into the vault of the temple. I had to keep the flame of my life burning. My eyes were ever vigil, my ears ultra-tuned. Being the chief priest's son, I had climbed those very steps countless times but tonight it was different. The warm inviting steps were cold and piercing. Something was telling me that I was not thinking straight. I willed myself to continue with the deed at hand. Desperate times called for desperate measures. And wasn't love the ultimate gift of God to mankind? With trembling hands, I had made sure that the crowbar rested near my armpit remained concealed. With equally trembling legs I had staggered across the steep steps of the temple. Anything for my love. Anything for him.

I was about to break the rusty lock of the door to the chamber housing the vault when I heard the muffled scream of Lata. Then everything else happened so fast that it was all a blur. I went home and explained everything to everyone. With tears rolling from her eyes Lata said that she regretted the marriage, a mistake as she had not made any attempt to understand who I really was. She told that she would divorce me and asked me to go to Vishal, sort his problems and get out of the country as the taboo would spit us out.

She advised me to call Vishal and tell him that I loved him. He needed and deserved to know. My mom pleaded and begged me to forget Vishal. My dad slapped me and said after much futile discussion that tonight was the day his son had died and asked me with folded hands to never show my face again in the village.

I had made up my mind and had to take a stand. I called Vishal and told him everything and that I was coming to meet him tomorrow. All he said was okay. That was all I needed. I packed my things in silence and collected what little money I had. Lata thrust some of her gold jewels into my hand and quickly disappeared sobbing. I promised myself to repay every bit of it and left my home. My father didn't come out of his room; I could hear Lata sobbing in the kitchen and my mom near the door, albeit crying didn't stop me.

* * *

I had taken the first available train to Bangalore and there I was in the rusty old train diverting myself in sweet kids and sour retrospect. I came back to reality as the train finally reached the destination. I had never been this anxious. With butterflies in my heart I travelled to Vishal's house in an auto and reached it after what seemed like an eternity.

There were many people near his house, and I had to make my way inside where I saw my love. For the last time. There he was lying on the floor with his broken neck. His throat had turned green and eyes were half protruding. The whole world was mute to me. A long sheet hung vertically from the now bent ceiling fan. I didn't feel sorrow. I didn't feel grief. I was just tired. Tired of losing. I couldn't save the man who had saved me. I had failed to instill hope in the man who had instilled faith in me. I sat beside him and caressed his cold cheek as tears started to roll down. I took one last look at the beautiful lifeless body whose soul I now own. He was then taken away, forever. I didn't protest. He deserved his peace. There was something written on the wall below his parents' photo. There were numerous interpretations running around, most saying that the message was for all the people he had cheated. But I knew it was for me and I would certainly honor it. He had sacrificed himself so that no other lives were ruined. I would not let my love go in vain. I started back to the station to my village, I would return the gold and money and meet my love again as the words filled my vision- 'I love you, but I am sorry. This is for you. Please forgive'. No one could stop love, not even life.

CHAPTER 9

"Isn't it weird how we take our body for granted?" said Supriya. "It takes a tiny dust mote in our eye, a dormant virus in our blood stream to realize just how vulnerable we all are."

"We willingly pollute and poison our system with all the filth in the world knowing very well that there was nothing before and there will be nothing after, this is what we have, a sack of flesh and bone to carry us around this beautiful blue spaceship," said Pierre Menard.

"Writer sir, please stop going on a tangent. We normal folks cannot keep up with you. But yes, it was horrible looking at people suffer in that rehabilitation center. The first-degree burns, spinal injuries, amputations. It was too much for me, but serving them was very helpful," said Avinash.

"Not to mention self-mutilation. Imagine, we would have occupied one of the beds there due to our own self harm incidents. There had to be someone to look after us all the while putting our near and dear ones in further misery," said Dhruv.

"Suicide is never the answer, but hey, who am I to judge? No one wants to die. They just want to kill the pain. But suicide doesn't kill the pain. It just passes to our loved ones," said Sharma.

"And no one remembers the person or the life you led before you committed suicide. All they remember is the end. Some say that you want to die because you were a failure. And if you survive after

 you try to commit suicide then you have failed in that too. That's brutal. But I think it is a much-needed shock to our system. A slap in the face. A vicious way to inspire and restart ourselves. As you said, suicide is like throwing a rock into a pond. We might drown but the repercussions travel around us, tarnishing our memory and transferring our sorrows in waves and wilting everything in its path, said Supriya, "due to the nature of my work, I have always seen death as my shadow. The dark silhouette who is never out of reach. He was this timid featureless being with hands and legs. But day by day, He started to grow intrepid. He started to nudge and crawl and sneak and creep up on me, always getting closer and closer. Till that one day, that fateful day, where He crossed the threshold and put His claw in me, reaching for my heart, corrupting it, sucking my urge, my desire, my right to live. The time has come to exorcise myself from him. To finally push him out of me and out of my life, to share my story and close my door on death."

CHAPTER 10

It was a restless night, again. Supriya Sinha had spent it twisting and turning on her double bed with the steady rain for company. Her thoughts were as relentless as the deluge outside which bombarded her with emotions that left a bitter taste in her mouth. The sky rumbled blithely, matching the light snoring of Supreeth Sinha, her stolid husband. It annoyed her that he could sleep peacefully, without a care about them. Some nights she felt as if a stranger had taken to her bed. They had gone to the same queen-sized bed every night for twelve long years from the day of their wedding. They had laughed together, cried together, planned and dreamt about their future together. Watched movies, read books, ate lazy dinners, recuperated when ill, made sweet love and slept huddled with each other on countless rainy nights like this.

The more they tried to get close, the more they had drifted apart, repelling one another. Everything had changed lately. There were no small talks, no innuendos, no date nights, no candle lit dinners; he trod on 'speak when spoken to' road and she played the part of the hapless and nagging house wife. Sex and intimacy had been a distant memory. Fights were common and usually took an ugly turn with her being the instigator more often than not. He didn't abuse or hit her, nor did he argue when confronted which further insulted her. It was as if she was not worthy of his rage. He was always calm, giving her the silent treatment to further her agony. She had too much time on her hand, too much freedom. Why doesn't he just talk to me? Where was all the love? Not knowing the answer to that made the bed grow small, suffocating and nauseating her.

Supriya stood up and stared out of the window tracing her fingers along the streams of water racing with each other on the other side. The dull night light on the other wall illuminated a framed picture of them together from their wedding reception.

The photo was reflected on the pane and the streams aligned on their smiling faces creating a morbid scene of tears rolling down their happy visage. Somehow, she felt that the tears suited her better than the frozen smile. She walked out of the soundless room filled with haunting screams of pain and taunting sneers.

She slowly entered the smaller room making sure the creaking door made no noise. On the single bed, snuggled among stuffed dolls and broken toys, within the soft blankets was her angel, her four-year-old son Sujay, sleeping peacefully. She sat on the edge of the cot and kissed her kid on the forehead. Sujay was the evidence that they had once been in love albeit he was conceived in a futile effort to save their crumbling marriage. He had held them together for four years, but she felt their days as a couple were numbered.

She knew the course ahead was not fair to her son which made her ill. Though her future looked bleak she cherished her past. She remembered the day they met vividly. It was the day of her 'retirement' from her very short tenure in the civil services whereas it was Supreeth's first day. They looked alike and their names were similar too, Supriya and Supreeth, names worthy of twin siblings. Love had blossomed from the very first day hidden among veiled glances and shy smirks. They had braved their families to be together, severed their blood ties to form their own which was sinewy at best now. The ringing of her cell- phone distracted her as she silenced it hurriedly. Sujay stirred and went back to sleep. She stared at the vibrating phone a long time before answering. It was her first love, probably her one true love, she thought.

The call was unexpected, quick and to the point. She turned around instinctively to check her surroundings and sensed a silhouette moving about. Dazed and confused, she went back to her room and saw that Supreeth was as she had left him. She checked her phone again before going to bed. This time sleep invaded her and sensing her stupor, Supreeth opened his eyes and spent the rest of the night blinking away his suspicions.

* * *

"Now where are you running off to?" said Supreeth to Sujay who jumped off his chair and ran towards his room almost running into Supriya who was carrying a plate of cut fruits, "He seems to be rather active today, almost eager to go to school."

"He is up to some mischief no doubt," said Supriya settling down on her chair at the breakfast table.

"You look… sharp. Any plans for the day?" said Supreeth sipping his coffee.

"Nothing in particular, need to shop for groceries," said Supriya miffed. Sharp was not the compliment any women would crave for but that was the most to hope from Supreeth.

"The blue scarf is a nice touch, goes with your eyes. Isn't that the present that I gave you when Sujay was born? You have to wear it more often."

"Yes, it is," said Supriya feeling uncomfortable. It was unlike him to notice her dress, to chit chat and remember meaningless presents. She got up from the table and moved towards the rooms, "I must check on Sujay. He will be late."

Why doesn't she just talk to me? thought Supreeth as he noticed Supriya's cell phone beside her plate. He didn't want to breach the threshold of trust that he had towards his wife, but yesterday's late-night call had changed that. Seeing her dressed in make-up this morning just to shop had further fueled his doubts, but he still couldn't reach across the table and take the phone from its comfortable niche. He stared at it as if it would turn to smoke and disappear, taking all his problems with it.

"You can look for your toys later. Finish your breakfast. Hurry," said Supriya as she carried Sujay and placed him on his chair and she settled in hers again to eat her fruits. Sujay sloshed his cereal around humming to himself for some time before running off again.

"Sujay!" screamed Supriya hurrying after him and addressing Supreeth, "Don't get up. Please, savor your coffee."

Supreeth took another sip ignoring the retort. He gulped his coffee down and strode to the bathroom and returned soon.

"You know why he kept running to his room? He was smuggling his water gun in parts, stuffing them in his back pack," said Supriya tying Sujay's shoe laces.

"I wanted to kill Ranjan," said Sujay pouting his lips, sad that his master plan was foiled, "He always plays with Suma more. She was my friend first."

"No guns to school. Try to be friends with Ranjan, and then all three of you can play together. You must learn to share, even your friends," said Supriya, "isn't it Supreeth?"

"Ah, yes. Share," said Supreeth vaguely trying to control his wrath over the disgusting taunt directed at him. Was he supposed to be OK in sharing her too? Using their child to affront him on this delicate matter showed how little she cared.

"Yes papa," said Sujay absently.

"Right then, off we go champ. Bye," said Supreeth to no one in particular as he picked Sujay up and went out the door with his laptop bag, closing it behind him.

* * *

Supriya parked her car on the upper basement near the exit and checked herself on the rearview mirror. The air was chilly and dry, but she perspired nonetheless. She dabbed at her face with a tissue and adjusted her perfect hair as she consciously checked the blinking digital clock mounted on the dashboard. She had enough time left ahead of her scheduled rendezvous, but it did little to calm her jittery nerves. She had planned her day perfectly, preparing the breakfast, organizing the lunch boxes, and dressing Sujay and drove to her destination after Supreeth and Sujay had left. She got off the car and walked towards the entrance of the mall without locking it. She made a mental note of her parking lot number and paced her steps as she entered through the metal detector. The mall was almost deserted at this time of the day in the early morning. Store owners, cleaning staff and security guards were more compared to the consumers. Students who had bunked their classes to watch the morning show and housewives with their overflowing shopping carts were scattered around like ants on the floor of the humungous glossy castle made of glass and granite. Supriya was one among them, emptying the contents of her cart into two large plastic carry bags, each time cross checking the crossed-out items from her lengthy groceries list. She carried them carefully, one on each hand, to the storage counter and dropped them there and collected a deposit stub. It was time.

Bruno Mars hummed listlessly from the speakers at Starbucks placed strategically at the corner of the ground floor arcade between the washrooms and entrance. Supriya ordered and paid for her black coffee to go and took the cup from the barista.

"Ah! Look at what you have done?" said the tall lady with the ever-growing coffee stain on her white salwar with elaborate golden embroidery.

"Oh, I am so sorry, really. I didn't notice you. Sorry," said Supriya as she placed her dripping, half spilt cup on the adjacent table, "don't wipe, it will smudge the stain further. There's a washroom next door, we will dab it with water."

"This was a gift you know, it will definitely leave a mark. You should be careful of your surroundings," said the lady in white as she hurried towards the toilet with Supriya in tow.

"I am sorry. I am ready to pay for the dry cleaning but let's try water first," said Supriya as she rushed beside her and entered the rest room almost colliding with the cleaning person coming out of the room.

"Great, it's stained," said the lady trying to dab at the brown blemish with tissue and water.

"Use a bit of that liquid soap," suggested Supriya as she walked to and fro. Just when the lady in white was about to protest, a glimmering lightning made an arc near her neck. She stepped back and blocked the slash with her wrist. Supriya had scanned the wash room when she entered but it wouldn't remain the same for long. Anytime now, someone would enter or worse, the lady in white could scream and call for help or run off. Supriya tried again, this time cutting her elbow and drawing blood. The lady in white, sensing the danger turned and tried to flee. Supriya caught her long and straight hair and yanked her back. She turned and tried to claw at her face. Supriya ducked under the sharp nails and stabbed her below the collar bone as her other palm cupped her mouth to muffle the cries.

"If you scream, I'll make it even more painful. Now, who, where and how?" said Supriya slowly taking her hand away from the mouth.

"I don't know what you are talking about."

The knife twisted. "Do you, now?"

"Starbucks at 10. Right corner seat, bald guy with a cane. You have to kiss him on his right cheek. He will give you a file which I'll have to give to someone else some other day. I don't know anything about that. That's all I know. Please."

The new knife brought from the store above did its job, as it pierced through cloth, skin and flesh. Supriya hugged the lady hard as she drove the knife further into her chest as the brown stain turned red and this time the lady in white did not complain. She wiped the knife clean with the tissue paper and hid it again as she had earlier. She placed the body on the toilet and locked the stall from inside. She stepped on the body and jumped over and out of the stall from the top and walked out. It was 9:58 AM.

She sat in the Starbucks café, sipping her coffee and staring out of the window. The knife now was lying next to her handbag, covered with her blue silk scarf as a bald guy with a sports cap sauntered towards her with a pronounced limp. He sat down at the corner seat across from her.

"You are late," said Supriya as she leaned over the table and kissed him on his right cheek.

"You are early," said the bald guy kissing her back and smelling her as he passed a big manila folder over the table. Her skin crawled as she flushed with disgust. She discreetly carried the folder masked by her bag and scarf with the knife and slowly went out of the café and collected her shopping bags.

Supriya had done just as she was ordered. The late-night call with its precise instructions was out of the blue. Being a sleeper agent for RAW had its shortcomings, but she knew that it was her first love, nation before anything else. She was recruited when she was working as a civil servant. Her retirement from the post was a front to keep her new job a secret. She kept her shopping bags in the back of the car when she felt a presence.

"You kissed me on the wrong cheek," said the bald guy pointing a silenced gun at her, "I had to tag you out of the mall to access my weapon because of the stupid detectors. I thought you will give me the slip, but I give you too much credit."

The bitch lied to me, thought Supriya.

"The folder please. It contains details of new recruits that I found for the Islamic State. Two years of work. You are mistaken if you think I will let you take it from me, that too a woman from the other side."

"Not just a woman, my wife," said Supreeth from behind the guy, swinging at his hand with his laptop bag.

Supreeth had scanned the call logs taking her phone to the bathroom. There was no incoming call registered at any time during the night. He had quickly replaced the phone in its original position. Clearly, the log was deleted, destroying the evidence which made him follow his wife. He had never dropped Sujay at school and instead tracked her going into the mall and inside Starbucks but losing her for some time when she went inside the washroom as Sujay was ogling at the chocolate fountain. He had to keep him occupied and not see his mother, for fear of him calling or running towards her. He saw her again entering the coffee shop and kissing a strange man. He thought both were leaving together somewhere, walking apart to avoid suspicion as he followed them out of the mall and into the parking.

But then he saw the guy drawing out a gun as he passed by a car and he had lunged instinctively with Sujay in tow.

Everything was then a blur. He could hear a faint click and a muffled gasp. The air rushed out of his lunges as the stranger's arm rammed into his midsection. He was pulled out as Supriya quickly twisted the bald guy's hand and wrenched the already smoking gun free and fired. The silenced weapon spit lead with barely a noise. Supriya didn't stop there. The gun fired again and again till the magazine emptied along with the skull of the bald man, but the firing went on and the blank clicks were deafening, and she collapsed slowly as she understood that her life had too. She could not even look behind her as she waited, waited for the scream, the wail and the sobs. It inevitably came; it was the final confirmation which she hoped to never have happened. She knew that was the end; of them. Supreeth was kneeling down cradling the now lifeless body of their four-year-old son Sujay. Supreeth's lunge had caused the shot aimed at her go haywire and hit her son right at his throat as he was running towards his parents. She knew that it was fatal. She would never forgive herself and neither would Supreeth. She sat there on the hard cement floor with myriad lights from parked cars filling the space and inquisitive and merciless eyes from strangers filled with judgment on the mother who had let her son die. To them, she was not a hero who had in all possibility, saved their lives, but a murderer, plain and simple. This would be noted lethargically in a confidential dust filled government file. Almost as a footnote, an afterthought that would state coldly that an agent suffered personal tragedy in the line of work. Collateral damage.

CHAPTER 11

"I never have worked so hard in my life," said Pierre Menard, "I have always believed that a healthy brain is enough to sustain my imagination. But I feel refreshed beyond compare. My mind feels unburdened. All my creative juices are flowing."

"I bet you will be singing a different song tomorrow when your body starts protesting," said an out of breath Avinash leaning on the parallel bars and looking upwards to the orange sky with a hint of blue in them threatening to break dawn.

"Don't get me down. I am too high with adrenaline to think of the repercussions," said Pierre doing jumping jacks on the grass beside the lone lemon tree which had small light green buds sprouting out of the crux of its most nascent leaves.

"Pierre, he is right. It is important to pace yourself. Don't let that lactic acid build up," said Supriya, "It is important to breath and relax. Come, sit with me and calm yourself."

"Not now yoga ma'am. After another run. What say Dhruv? Up for a race?" said Pierre.

"I used to hike to my temple which was above hundred and seventy steep, stone steps, on a small hill, twelve times every day, for around fourteen years. I have had my exercise, it is time to strengthen my mind. Meditation is my game now."

"Scared of losing to a guy twice your age, I get it. What about you Sharma? Same age will even the playing field. Or you too want to take the pussy way out and 'introspect'?" said Pierre looking at others mockingly.

"Fine, someone has to shut you up," said Sharma.

"Go Sharma. If I win, you will have to tell your story. You know that it is inevitable. You are the last one left," said Pierre.

"Hey, come on. That's not fair. There will not be any judgement. If someone doesn't want to share, then it is up to them," said Supriya.

"I am just incentivizing that's all. All he has to do is beat me," Said Pierre raising his hands in mock surrender.

"Hmmm. All right. Only beating you will shut you up. So, let's begin," said Sharma.

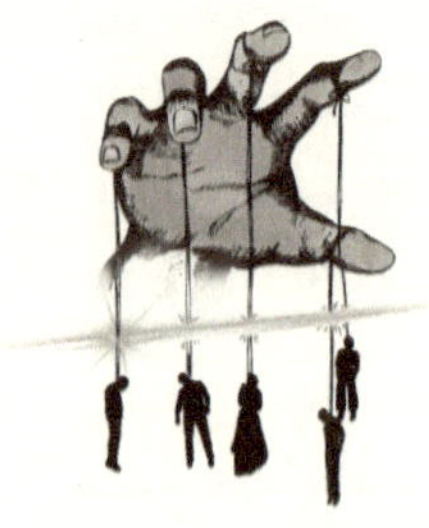

CHAPTER 12

The room was vast and gloomy. Huge venetian blinds covered the giant windows stretching half way to the ground. Streams of light danced from within the strips casting eerie and strange shadows on the large wooden table. The wall adjacent to the windows had a notice board with various news articles pinned to it. Next to it hung a framed doctor's license and a family photo. Below it was a shiny life-sized mirror. The eloquent and elaborate carvings on its panes were covered with a fine film of dust. The big office desk was sturdy and made of pinewood, littered with papers, files and divided the room. A laptop and a big digital clock with blinking numbers sat on the corner of the desk. A framed photo of a young, smiling woman was obscured at the other corner. Straight and uncomfortable oak chairs with leather seats stood sentry on either side of it.

"Thank you for seeing me on such short notice Doctor Sharma," said Rajesh as he stood fidgeting next to the visitor's chair, contemplating whether to sit or not. He stood with his head bowed low, as if afraid to make eye contact, "Umm, sorry for barging in. I… I… I know you don't see any one without a prior appointment. But thanks again for making an exception." His hair was rough and undone and his dress shabby, wearing an overcoat too large for his size. With bloodshot eyes he saw the clock strike 8 p.m.

"Not to worry. You have been my long-time patient, no need to apologize," said Doctor Sharma adjusting his finely oiled thick hair in the mirror and gesturing his patient to take a seat. He was a young-looking man dressed immaculately in double pressed formals. He himself sat down and ran through the files on his desk and fished out a rather large red file and skimmed through it, "It seemed rather urgent. Besides, would you have turned down your patient?"

"I certainly wouldn't have. But I am not a doctor anymore," said Rajesh smiling sheepishly slouching from his seat, and then continued more seriously, "I am not ready Sharma. No. No. Not at all. I thought I was. You thought I was. But no, I… I… am not ready to face it. Face… her…."

"Rajesh, this is common. Guilt is a relentless pursuer. But it's a good thing; it means you have a conscious," said Sharma in an assuring tone sitting ramrod straight with his elbows on the arm rest and his palms interlocked, "You have suffered enough. Mistakes do happen, and tragedies ensue."

"But, the things I have done. Has anything changed?"

"Hmm, these doubts and questions are good. You are thinking about others. Let's recant a bit, shall we? Will help you realize how far you have come; how hard you have fought."

"I guess these thoughts were never..."

"Mmhhmm, you know the rules. Always start from the first. Tell me what happened in the beginning which made you come here. Emotional recursion," said Sharma enunciating half mockingly and holding up a hand, interrupting Rajesh, "Hell, you developed this technique Doctor Rajesh."

"Have you ever had any success with my technique with other patients?" asked Rajesh meekly.

"Sure, yes. Absolutely" said Sharma hesitatingly adjusting his perfectly placed hair.

"You never were a good liar Doctor Sharma. Don't know how you succeeded as a psychiatrist," said Rajesh returning the mock.

"It's a damn powerful technique. Hearing yourself talk about your problems will help in understanding the situation more clearly as you relive it again. It will no doubt bring clarity to both of us."

"I... Yes, trying my technique on myself. Will get to know what it is to be on the other side of the table. Actually, that might just be what I need; a good listener. It will be easier for you to analyze it too. To tell me I am over-thinking."

"Yes, most times you will feel that there was no problem to begin with, that you just needed an assurance. So, let's start again, from the beginning, Raju.

* * *

"Raju," repeated Rajesh pulling his left ear twice, "It... it's been a while since I heard my name like that. Raaaju." He gestured a backhand motion as he slowly stretched the name, savoring its sound with his eyes closed, "My mother used to call me that. She never used to call me by my full name. Never. She was repulsed by my full name. Considered it to be sacrilegious to utter it. Blasphemous!"

"I have to ask, as Shakespeare once famously asked, what's in a name?"

"You see, I was christened by my father. She didn't want anything that had his stamp. Though she didn't show it, deep down, I knew she had a nurturing hatred towards me too; but luckily, I was half her, so she had to care for me."

"I guess everything, and I mean everything starts from mothers."

"No… No… I am not blaming her. My dad, he was never around. An alcoholic, wannabe writer. I never saw him holding a pen. Writing was neither his vocation nor avocation. Drinking was his inspiration and gambling his motivation to hurt me and my mother. So, her hatred was well justified. I am surprised she didn't kill him."

"So, she suffered in silence?"

"She was quite liberated. She fought hard to get a divorce. That broke me," said Rajesh pulling at his ear, "Not the divorce per se. I was 8 years old. I remember listening to her on the phone, telling her sister, my aunt, that she was devastated because she had deprived her son of a father figure. That's when I vowed that if ever, I had a child I wouldn't let this happen."

"You see, you showed a great amount of maturity at that young age."

"I had this thing, where I shrunk or prolonged time in my mind. If I was scolded and beaten by my father for half an hour, I would imagine it only happened for a minute, really helped me cope with the sadness. It's a huge part of Emotional Recursion too. Actually, it is the whole basis of it. Stuff your problems in a time capsule and poof... Forget it."

"Or imagine that something bad which recently happened has happened in the past, not bothering you in the present. Yes, controversial coping mechanism but effective nonetheless. Then…?"

"My mother wanted to fill that void my dad had left, emotional and financial, with a string of boyfriends, none seriously trying. She never did marry again."

"There were a couple of horrible choices too, I believe."

"Oh yes. There was one who wanted to be an actor. He used to enact his small scenes in front of me. I learned to act, to mask my emotions from him. And then there was the drunk post-man. I believe he was fed up of just giving things to others, so he started taking things from others too. He used to steal from my mother and my mother from him. Later, he was arrested stealing from his own post-office. There were other specimens too, rich and poor, good and bad, left and right. It was because of them that I was able to complete my education and grow my personality."

"In retrospect, they were critical in your upbringing."

"Absolutely. Also, my mother was a miser, very careful with money. She always used to tell- Yaavad vitto parjana shakthaha| Staavannija parivaaro rakthaha||"

"Yes. Till the moment you are fit to earn money, your family is in love with you. So true. From Baja Govindam by Adi Shankaracharya, if I am not wrong. Your mother was a very wise woman."

"Indeed, she was. The only thing she wanted was for me to earn money. Money demands respect."

"Hmm, didn't this affect your education? Having no money, struggling and dreaming about getting rich?" said Sharma adjusting his hair.

"On the contrary, it motivated me. I was a nerdy, dorky geek at college. Immersed in my books," said Rajesh pulling at his ear twice, "Girls never went with guys like me. They preferred ball players, athletes. People like Sajid."

"Sajid?"

"He was the popular kid in college. Tall and handsome. I was in awe of him. The way he carried himself, the way he spoke. I always wanted to be like him. I would imitate his actions every morning in front of my mirror."

"Good. It develops confidence, nothing wrong in being confident."

"In fact," said Rajesh chuckling, "you look strikingly similar to Sajid. The resemblance is uncanny."

"I guess that's a compliment. What about Sajid then?"

"He was popular not because he was brilliant, but because he was filthy rich. Even teachers respected him. That's the main reason why I pursued medicine; psychiatry. A respectable profession and financially sound. At least, that's what I thought, no offence.

"None taken," said Sharma calmly.

"I had a nice practice Doctor Sharma. Finally, I had some money. I met a beautiful girl, Renuka. I first saw her when I was presenting my paper in a college. There were three hundred people in the room and my eyes could comprehend only her. I thought I was in love. I knew then that I had to marry her to fulfill my mother's prophecy for me. A successful man must have a beautiful wife. I thought accomplishing that grand plan would bring contentment."

"So, you succeeded then, in your endeavor?"

"I did. Surprisingly, it wasn't that hard to convince her to marry me. Money Power. I knew she was marrying me for my money, but I didn't complain. Then, I lost my mother," said Rajesh, "She had suffered silently for 8 long years."

"That must have been too hard for you."

"I am ashamed to say no. Even the death of my mother didn't affect me. You see, I was living in a trance. It was my time to be happy. I had fulfilled her dream. Her dying was not part of the plan. If I had been sad then she would be too. Moreover, that's the time when Ruhi was born."

"A roller coaster of a ride, emotionally draining," said Sharma in a tone hinting at sadness.

"Yes. I remember holding my angel for the first time. She was so small and delicate. She was like a lump of dough, all pink and tender. I didn't pick her till she was a year old, afraid that I will drop her," said Rajesh mimicking the action of holding a baby in his arms.

"That's natural, a protective love of a dedicated father."

"Yes, I was a proud father. I finally came out of my hangover when Ruhi was around five years old. I saw Renuka hitting her because she refused to drink a glass of milk. That's when I missed my mother the most. It was a common scene, a mother disciplining her adamant child. But these things started happening again and again. Renuka used to take her anger on me out on innocent Ruhi," explained a melancholic Rajesh gloomily.

"What happened there?"

"Ruhi became a whipping child for me. Young prince and princess used to have kids who used to be beaten when they misbehaved. You see, you can't hit royal kids, so you hurt them through guilt. That's when reality dawned on me. I couldn't love someone who would hit my child. Not even the mother of my child," said Rajesh with his voice rising at each passing sentence.

"Tell me about your wife. How was she?"

"She required a lot of upkeep. Her shopping, her parties, her spa sessions, her frequent trips, she had her dreams, her desires. She was not the kind of a person to adapt and adjust. She was high maintenance," said Rajesh in a halting and measured tone.

"How did you provide for all these?"

"I broadened my client base. I started therapy sessions for

Rohit."

"Ah! Rohit. A star at a very young age. Couldn't handle the stardom, and resorted to drug abuse, destroying his future. Classic, but that didn't go well I suppose."

"Not at all, Rohit was mad."

"Hey, wasn't it Carl Jung who said everyone is insane? Show me a sane man and I will cure him for you."

"Yes, yes. Everything was fine. I tried my technique on him. He couldn't handle the trauma. To help him, I had to give him an anti-depressive agent which was very quick acting. It was not yet approved. But I was sure of it. Besides, I was offered a huge amount by the pharmaceutical, if I treated using the drug," said a forlorn Rajesh.

"Oh god," said Sharma adjusting is in-place hair.

"The medicine was working, but Rohit screwed up. The idiot had had a shot of heroin along with it. He O.D.ed and died," said Rajesh in a maudlin tone as he pulled at his ear.

"And that's the reason you lost your practice, your doctor's license was cancelled. You had to sell your house to fill the lawyer's cost and pay the fine."

"Yes," said Rajesh nodding, "Years of hard work gone. What little savings I had vanished. I had to borrow heavily to pay out the fine and legal fees. I was finally cleared of the charge of killing the idiot. But yes, I am not a doctor anymore after just 8 years of practice. After all this, when I came to my clinic to have a bit of peace, my wife came, demanding divorce. The one thing which I had promised myself that I wouldn't let happen."

"All this, when you most needed her to be on your side," said Sharma shaking his head disapprovingly.

"I... I... remember the day as though it was today, like it happened just now. She was screaming at me, saying that she couldn't wait to get away from me. She would make sure that I would not see my daughter again. That was the trigger, I guess, but I didn't know when or how, but my hands were clasped around her throat," said Rajesh with his voice quivering and crumpling the paper in front of him, "She was struggling, suffocating. I liked it. When I realized what I was doing, she was long gone. I was holding the neck of my dead wife."

"What has happened has happened" said Sharma pushing the glass of water across the table for him to drink, "Freud said, 'the goal of all life is death'. You have paid your debts to the society. It's time for you to take responsibilities, to face your fear. You have repented enough. Ruhi needs you. You are all she's got. Remember, you went through this turmoil so that you can be there for her, to take care of her."

"I... I know. She is the only reason that I am alive. She is my purpose. You know, she turns 8 today. I can't let her down," said Rajesh pulling at his ear and sitting straight, "I can't let her down like I let others down. That's what scares me. But yes, listening to my story cleared some things. I did everything for her, but I couldn't provide an unbroken home. But now, I must take care of her."

"Good. You see, your technique works," said Sharma

slouching in the chair and pulling at his ear twice, "Go to her. Take… take care of her."

"Thanks doctor Sharma, all this happened what, 8 years ago? It's ridiculous to worry about it still. My technique indeed works. Thanks. I will take care of her." said Rajesh adjusting his rough hair into place by looking himself in the mirror and getting up smiling and shaking his hands in the air. He is greeted by the empty chair across the table as the clock strikes 8:08 p.m.

He took out a strip of tablets from his pocket and pops a couple of pills. He slowly walked through the room and glanced at the picture of him with Renuka and Ruhi, all smiles and happy. He lightly caressed his daughter and read the license beside it with a sigh. The glass was cracked, and the name was torn apart. He proceeded to read the assorted highlighted newspaper clippings pinned to the board where different headlines read:

DOCTOR RAJESH SHARMA TREATING WITH UNAPPROVED MEDICINE, ARRESTED

ACTOR ROHIT FOUND DEAD, FOUL PLAY HINTED. PSYCHIATRIST'S LICENSE REVOKED

SAJID WINS WORLD BILLIARDS CHAMPIONSHIP AGAIN

Rajesh Sharma then moved away from the wall and out of the room carefully stepping aside the corpse of his wife beside the door, the same lady in the picture on the desk beside the red file marked as 'Self-Diagnosis'. The other wall had details about his technique and 'TAKE CARE' scribbled all over the empty spaces. 'KILL HER TO TAKE CARE' was written in bold at the bottom.

* * *

The evening news reader reported the trials and tribulations of Doctor Rajesh Sharma:

Renowned psychiatric doctor, Rajesh Sharma was found unconscious at his wife's place. He most likely had attempted suicide by sleeping pills. The body of his 8-year-old daughter was found nearby. The body of his wife, Renuka was recovered from his office. Both allegedly strangled to death by Rajesh Sharma before trying to commit suicide. Police are speculating it to be a case of double murder and are investigating on the reason. Dr. Sharma had a brush up with the law earlier too for his controversial treatment for celebrity Rohit which ended badly....

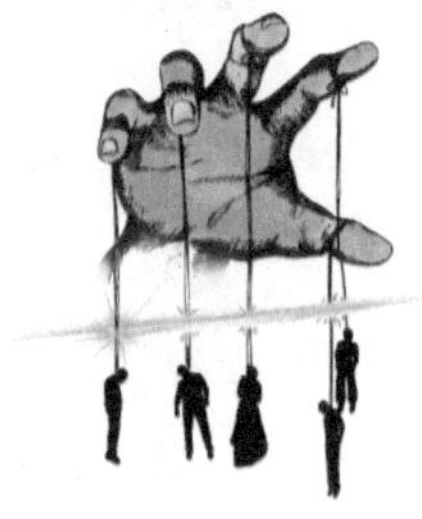

CHAPTER 13

There was a hush after Rajesh Sharma told his story. It was done. End of the road. Now everyone knew who the others really were. They had laid bare their life. No embellishments, and no watering down their tales. All five had been open and sincere in their retelling. Judgement be damned. It was a long pause, a pregnant silence but it was not uncomfortable, it was the contented calm that comes with close family and best friends. Pierre stood up and with a slight hesitation walked towards his room and shut the door. Slowly, all the others followed suit, each going into their own quarters and closing the door.

After a lengthy while, with clockwork precision, all five of them emerged. And all of them came out with their belongings nicely packed in their respective luggage. Each of them stood in the threshold stupefied to see others who had come to the same decision. Finally, it was Rajesh who spoke.

"I did not realize that there is sweetness in losing. Sweetness because you learn from it. Sweetness because you overcome it. And sweetness because you are better because of it. Thank you, Pierre. I probably needed that push to let go of my inhibitions. I know Aman from before. From my days of practicing. But now I understand his process. I was embarrassed to go to my colleague for a court mandated therapy after my… er… after the killing of my wife and my daughter, for which I have served my time. But he has shown me the light. There is still a taboo associated with mental sickness and I being a psychiatrist failed to understand my own psyche. I will help others. I will teach, publish and counsel. I will not let what happened to me happen to others."

"A hundred times yes. Like you guys said so benevolently after hearing to my story, it is time for me to come out of my cocoon and try to fly again. Though my prison sentence was dismissed I was not exonerated, I do not have money for an appellate court. The defamation case is misused by the rich where exorbitant sums are included to scare the opposition. I mean, how can you quantify dignity? How can you fix an amount which equates to a person's self-esteem? It should not change depending on the social status. But I digress. Though I joined therapy because it was court mandated, I am glad that I did. I will use a pseudonym. I will not think about the past. I can still prove my originality. My dream is not dead, it is just unwell, and writing is just the nourishment it needs. Writing is what is required to gain respect, to gain back my wife and kid. I am ready," said Pierre.

"Yes. That's the way to go. It applies for all of us. I have lost my wife, my friend. I have served time. The court mandated therapy after knowing about my selective memory loss was the best thing that could have happened to me. I can drown in the guilt or overcome it and start afresh and live for the love that I have lost," said Avinash.

"I might have lost my love, but I will live in the shade of its warm memory. I might have joined this psyche program because of my parents' insistence as the guilt of ruining a young girl's life bore down my resolve. They think my sexual orientation is a disease. But they inadvertently have helped me. I will help others who are ostracized for just loving. I will fight for equality," said Dhruv.

"I served my country and lost my family. I lost my child and my husband has remarried. I had to take psyche evaluations to ascertain my fitness to get back into duty, though it will be nothing but a desk job. But I faltered and lost my way where I craved for the sweet release of death. Victim blaming must be shunned but it is useless playing the victim card. My actions that day resulted in saving hundreds of kids. I see my baby in them and shall live to safe guard their future too. Once a mom, always a mom right, "said Supriya.

With that, after a very long and forgotten time, they all smiled. They smiled with no inhibition, they smiled with no guilt pulling them down, they smiled from the heart and felt its warmth too, they smiled for each other, to acknowledge and validate their collective decision, but most importantly, they smiled for themselves. They smiled for the lives and love lost, they smiled for their grim past, their turbulent present but more so for their bright future. And so, they left seeking solace and a new beginning....

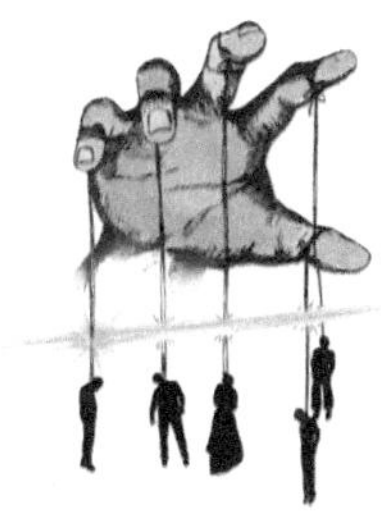

CHAPTER 14

Four years ago
Central Jail, Bangalore

Yazdaan Abbas always felt that there was a wave like property to the prison complex. The pandemonium of the highway traffic was the crest and the uncomfortable hush that fell as soon as you enter the intimidating walls was the trough. As you signed your visitation record and enter with the visitor's pass after getting thoroughly searched, the crest soon began again with the meeting chambers, where there were often the deflated cries on one side of the glass barricade and muted sighs and sobs from the other. The trough soon followed as you entered the internal waiting chamber. This is where he felt the most vulnerable. The wait. He was always afraid of the time before his meet with someone, it mattered little if he knew the person he was meeting or not. He tended to overthink too much and that added to his acute apprehension. He always longed for the next crest. The actual inside of the prison complex, the belly of the beast. He looked at the time on his black battered HMT Janata watch by feeling the worn belt, finding some solace in its soothing, memory saturated touch. Finally, after a long wait, he was ushered into the crest. Though he was surrounded by hardened criminals with no vindication in sight, the constant chirping of the inmates eased his taut nerves. With some guilt, that is what he imagined it to be. Chirping way their songs of sorrow. Birds with their feathered wings clipped, chirping in agony, yearning for freedom, craving to fly in the clear blue sky, but knowing deep within that they will not feel the wind caressing their tear dried cheeks again. Prison system was just barbaric cages made to hold animals, a corrupt bureaucratic system which thrived on maintaining the status quo, a criminal must and should remain a criminal. Rehabilitation here was a joke.

He then entered a small meeting room, for the final trough, reserved for a personal tête-à-tête for lawyers meeting their high-profile clients or convicts requiring therapy or in very rare cases, conjugal visitation for the privileged inmates. To alleviate his trepidation, he started to peruse through his files knowing very well that it wouldn't. Today was a big day. No more procrastination. Instinctively, his fingers sought his watch and started caressing it.

There was a loud buzz and the door opened and in walked a prisoner dressed in regulation ill stitched loose white cotton shirt and trouser. He was not restrained, and the constable nodded to the inmate while giving Yazdaan an expressionless stare before exiting from the room and locking it from the outside. The prisoner, Yazdaan knew, was in his late fifties but surprisingly looked much younger. It seemed that prison life had suited him. The spread of salt and pepper hair and the lean build added certain nuance to his apparent maturity, showing that he was doing well, but the slight tilt in his shoulders when he stood still, and his deep boring eyes said a different story altogether. There was too much tension in his shoulder blades and the bloodshot eyes, crow's feet in its corner and the ever-increasing dark circles beneath signaled that he was a troubled man. Yazdaan Abbas stood and greeted his visitor by shaking his hands, with a smile on the faces of both which neither felt.

"I still haven't gotten used to our little arrangement here," said Dr. Rajesh Sharma as he sat across Yazdaan on a small wooden chair with no arm rests. There was a wooden table carved with crass graffiti in between. There was a low cot in the corner with a musky quilt filled with myriad stains.

"How so Dr. Rajesh?" said Yazdaan.

"Come on Yazdaan," said Rajesh, "this is not the first time we are having this discussion. If we have to move further, then you have to let go. This right here is a classic example, always starting our conversation by clinging to the formality and addressing me as 'sir' or by adding 'Dr.' in front of my name, even after asking you not to many times, it shows that you are not ready to let go. You only accept the norm after I insist every time that you do. If we need to make any progress, then you need to relent. Sometimes a ship can only survive the storm if the anchor is cut loose."

"True. I apologize Rajesh. I have to let go," said Yazdaan, running his fingers on the uneven surface of the belt of his watch.

Rajesh made a mental note of it. He had acknowledged this movement many times during their past visits. Time was running, and his visitor acknowledged it. For whom the bell tolls?

"And what you said probably answers your query I suppose. A psychiatrist is coming in to the prison for therapy, to take counselling from an inmate. Ah, the irony. But the inmate is a renowned psychiatrist himself."

"Was," corrected Rajesh.

"I believe that knowledge can never be lost. Licenses and legality might change but possessed information gained from experience can never perish. You taught us in college. You are teaching me now. That's it."

"I was just a guest faculty for a semester Yazdaan. And that was, what, ten years ago?"

"That was enough for you to make a mark on us. That's why I am here. That's why I sought you and fought to meet you here. At this place."

"I commend your viciousness. Not just getting the court order but convincing me too. Person who perseveres persists. I admit that keeping appearances has its own thrill, what with others thinking that I am the one who is undergoing therapy."

"That was the only way I could be here. And I fully acknowledge how difficult it must have been for you in the inside. I know seeking therapy, though as a ruse, is frowned upon here, both by the guards and by the fellow inmates. They think it is less manly."

"Not less, but not manly at all. Period. The world still thinks that a man has no right to show his emotions. But, enough digressing. You know you cannot keep stalling me. We are on a fixed timeline here. At least, I am," said Rajesh gesturing to the windowless walls around. "So, Yazdaan, are you ready?"

"Yes. This time, I am. And I know, always start from the first", said Yazdaan, keeping his files on the small rudimentary table so that he was somewhat obscured from Rajesh's vision, a small barricade to shield from the judgmental eyes but then, after a slight hesitation, pushed it to the side and immediately grabbed his left wrist where his watch was.

Rajesh gave a knowing yet subtle, non-critical nod. The anchor was cut.

CHAPTER 15

"But abu, it was him who started it. He took my drawing and tore it," Yazdaan Abbas said as he held on to his father's hand. The school bag was a little too big for his stature. He had to hustle after every step to keep up with the pace of his father. The late autumn sun was begrudgingly climbing through the snow-capped mountains as if awakened in the middle of a deep slumber dreaming of peace in the valley.

"Yazdaan, my noor chai," said Yawaar Abbas kneeling beside his son and holding him in his upper arm, "You are a big boy now. There will always be someone looking into other's life. Other's happiness, other's talent will always bring focus to their lack of it. They will not be able to control the feeling that comes with it. And when that feeling is left alone, it slowly turns sour and bad just like anything. The spoilt emotions will then burn, fueling their rage and they will direct it towards those who outperform them. That's jealousy. You have to be the bigger man. Agreed, you have to deal with the bullying. But beating them until they bleed will only add to their misery and it will not get your drawing back."

"He tore my drawing of your watch. The one which you have promised to give to me."

"I completely understand. But bodily harm is seen as a severe offence than emotional harm. Understand and always remember this. We will make a pact with each other now. Always be good and do good. Peace will follow you. Never expect anything from anyone," said Yawaar, then sighed and continued, "Oh well… I too must remember that you are just six years old. Just remember to have your sad face on when you apologize to the Head Master and the boy's parents. That's the only way you can stay in school and not get expelled. All right?"

"Yes. So, is my birthday still cancelled?"

"Hey, that's not my department. You have to talk to your ammi about it. But I will put in a good word for you. But don't expect whole wazwan to be prepared in your honor."

"Thanks, abu. And abu, stop calling me your noor chai. At least not near my school," said Yazdaan glancing sideways to look at his dad's wristwatch. A shiny black strap holding the HMT Janata timepiece.

"Look at Mr. Grown-up here. One minute he wants his baby birthday and the next he orders his abu. All right big man. How does Yazdaan sir sound? And stop looking at my watch. You will have other watches, but this is still mine for another fifteen years at least. Remember, you have to pass your graduation in first class. You have to earn it."

"I will abu."

"This was given to me by my abu. I earned it too. It was a rite of passage, proving that you are a man now. And speaking of watches, look at the time," said Yawaar, "Sorry Yazdaan sir, I have to carry you and run if we are to keep you from getting expelled."

"You cannot lift me abu," said Yazdaan laughing as he was hoisted over his father's waist.

"We might have had to wait sixteen long years to have you, but my legs are still strong enough to carry my noor chai," said Yawaar as he jogged through the grassy knoll towards Sopore primary school.

That was the last day that I was carried by my father. At some point, parents will put their kids down without knowing that they will never pick them up again. Many people view this as a tragedy but knowing exactly when that happened is infinitely sadder. Abu lost his legs when he threw himself at the IED which he had uncovered by accident. A school bus would have passed over it and would have torn it into pieces due to the bus's fuel tank. He singlehandedly saved all the life on that bus. Thirty-three kids getting ready for their matriculation and the driver. He lost part of his stomach and large intestine. The shrapnel pieces in his spine made him a paraplegic for life. There were third degree burns on his chest and neck. My mother was completely lost in taking care of him and rightly so. Suddenly, I saw the valley as others saw it. To me it was just my home. My own personal heaven. Now I saw the fire. The conflagration moving through the hills and trees and finally consuming people in its flames fueled by jingoism and pride. There is a saying in the valley:

Akya tshod duniya ti beyi akya yiman,

duniya ti yimaan chini dunivay athi yivan.

One man sought the world, and another sought for faith,

The world and faith both do not go hand in hand.

My paradise was burning, and we were all timbers to be fed into it. The only loser in a perpetual tug of war is the rope. Tragedy has a nice way of stripping the innocence of a child, isn't it?

The still burning embers of the explosion formed the spotlight under which we were put under. My dad was a hero, but he was celebrated only to further their own motives than to honor his bravery. We did not need their sympathy, we needed assurance that this would not happen to others, we needed a guide to direct us through our murky future. He was paraded across all the television channels. Tabloids carried his picture under incendiary articles. His return to work was hailed and exalted. There were many awards but no rewards. And pretty soon, just like the numerous garlands with which he was felicitated, the limelight wilted and disappeared into non-existence along with my father. A hero forgotten, sidelined by the system that the society operates in. He was just another imbecile, crippled and neglected.

As the seasons changed and years passed, our struggle kept increasing. We were left in perpetual autumn, waiting for our spring. But we only saw the cold dead nights of winter ahead. The office gave him the pink slip without any preamble. They had endured enough of my father's PTSD. After all, they had a business to run.

There was no severance or pension paid as he was deemed unfit to work. Both physically and mentally. When a family loses income, they quickly lose their relatives and friends too, afraid that they will be called in to help. Various loans from pawnbrokers came short of the mountainous medical bills of my father. Ammi and my work as laborers barely kept a roof over our head and food in our belly. All the charities blatantly said that their publicity was done for the year, with some or the other natural calamity. You see, helping one person will not bring them any P.R. Government shut their door on us, with what them belonging to a right-wing conservative party inclined towards Hindu hardliners. Them helping us, a religious minority with election around the corner was just out of the question, even if the elections were four years away. And all through this, my abu shrank further down his shriveled shell.

Off all the misery that we had endured, getting rebuked by the very people he had saved was the most gruesome. We did not know that abu had gone ahead and found out about each one of the survivors all by himself. All of them, now having or starting to have a family of their own, in their personal throes of adulthood. We did not know that he had gone to them asking and pleading for help. He was cast aside as a leper. Many did not even acknowledge his presence, and some had forgotten about him. That was the tipping point. And you know the rest.

He sent them all a fake electronic invite to commemorate the tenth-year anniversary of the horrid event, a toast to their survival, all under the pretense of allegedly being sponsored by a benevolent NGO. He even paid the private cable channels to promote the event in their ticker tape in the Sopore area and booked a small convention hall and we were horribly unaware of all of this. We were oblivious to the firecrackers and petrol cans that were stashed under the satin cloth draped chairs in the hall that fateful morning. He had carefully bought them through various bunks and stores and stashed them at our house weeks prior to the date. He had rigged a small can of petrol spiked with zinc, sulfur and cordite under his wheel chair which he detonated on the day which was coincidentally a Sunday, which increased the crowd. The petrol cans fueled the explosion, killing the very people he had saved along with many others. Pregnant woman and kids were charred to death. Old and young alike were robbed of their future and a hero had become a villain. In the end, my father, my abu had become a terrorist.

I identified the body of my father by the HMT Janata watch that he was wearing. It was still ticking, and it still is. As promised, I never wore that watch until I graduated, until I earned my doctoral degree. One of the survivors said that the dying words of my abu was that he had died ten years ago. He had died trying to save the ungrateful people by sacrificing his family. True, there was one victim in that IED blast all those years ago, the unfortunate thing was that the victim had survived. I know it might seem harsh but that is the reality. My dad should have died a hero. Our world is too harsh towards the needy. We were shunned from the society, outcast and unofficially exiled. Even when we were poor, we had our pride, now we had none. But still, we held our heads high but had to relocate. The sins of the father are visited upon the children. With perseverance and patience, I earned a benefactor and struggled through my education. My father always used to tell me to be good and do good and not expect anything from anyone. In return or otherwise and peace would follow. We made a pact. We made a Ulysses Pact. If only he held on to it. This is what drove me to psychiatry. And this is why I am here.

CHAPTER 16

Present day
Somewhere in Bangalore

The camera stream rolled on, focusing on dead and empty spaces. The angles, focus and views changed as the editors tried to do something until the stream was cut. Over the past few weeks, the house which was specially modified to record and track its inhabitants was abuzz with activity but now the cameras saw only stagnant furniture and recorded dead silence. And then, abruptly, everything faded to black with a '500 Internal Server Error' message.

The night was slowly starting to turn turbulent. The speckles of stars were grudgingly blanketed by lazy clouds. The dark night developed the dangerous blue hue which signaled the oncoming deluge. Yazdaan waited for some time and refreshed his browser. The same error message appeared. With a sigh, he closed the window and opened another encrypted portal to verify that everything was in order. Everything was. That's it. It was done. He couldn't believe that he had pulled it off. His experiment was complete.

After some hours of exasperated activities which needed his utmost attention, he sat down finally with nothing else to do. The knock on the door startled Yazdaan. He expected visitors but not the ones who would knock and not this soon. Hesitantly, he stood up and made his way through the darkness and looked into the peep hole. He stood at the door with indecision and then opened the door before there was another knock which might ruin his tranquility. As if incensed by the silence, the sky broke up with a thunder.

Dr. Rajesh Sharma sat in front of Yazdaan like the many occasions that they had, many years ago. The only difference was, this time, Rajesh was looking for answers. A mild table lamp lit the space between them casting huge shadows all around.

"So, this is the lemonade stand from which Lucy is disbursing psychiatry," said Rajesh.

"No wonder you got the Charlie Brown and the tree reference," said Yazdaan looking through the window where there was now a continuous spatter of the rain drops.

"Well… there was only one tree in the yard at the 'house'. A single lemon tree and you had informed me in the prison on your final visit that if I wanted, when everything was done, I should have peanut with Lucy. I didn't know there was place called The Lemonade up for rent for very short durations in the city."

"Yes… there are many such establishments which offers retreat for creative folks. Writer's retreat, yoga retreat, spiritual awakenings and such. It suited well for me and was available. The 'house' too was one such establishment which I got modified for our... er... experiment. I didn't know that you would drop by... after everything...."

"Why wouldn't I? Life's too short to learn only from your own mistakes. You changed me Yazdaan. You changed all of us. You instilled hope. You saved us. You gave us life."

"Come on Doc. You saved yourselves. I was just the catalyst. I had to take a risk on this unethical social experiment. A risk on myself and five other life. Objectively speaking, I considered myself lucky even if one of you survived. And to be very frank, the odds on that was negligible."

"Even if I don't agree with the approach, I understand the thought process. I have two questions for you. How did you pull this off? I know the science of it, though controversial, but I want to know the logistics behind it. The funding and the operations and second, what do the numbers on the file mean?"

"The principle is simple Rajesh. Overton Window. You just have to find the audience. They are always there."

"Like rule34 on the internet."

"Exactly, if it exists, there is porn of it."

"So, Overton Window. You applied a concept of political science to psychiatry which basically says that there is a window of ideas that a public is willing to accept and everything outside is radical or downright ridiculous."

"Yes, when you have to shift the window of acceptability, you have to start at the extreme. Say or present something ridiculous so that the radical seems standard or ordinary. You are shifting the *Overton Window*. Now, the radical is the new normal. This has been happening over a course of time. Look around you. The powers that be are manipulating us to shift the window to suit their agenda. I didn't shift the window. It was already shifted and to extremes. I just exploited it through the Deep Web. Over the years, I learnt some concepts of IT networking, programming, cryptocurrencies, internet securities and stock trading and banking. This helped me in my setup. There are other more despicable and sinister things going on with even higher production value and astronomical investments. I just found my niche and milked them and to answer your second question, skimmed the cream."

"I doubt if I understand Yazdaan. This takes a giant leap from reality with a willing suspension of disbelief. But, red pill me here."

"As I had laid out to you, I needed you not just for your betterment but as a moderator to steer the others according to the protocol. You were a psychiatrist and knew some part of the trial. You were my unblinded subject in the study, my ace in the hole. I used the wonders of the internet to live stream the happenings at the house as a 'reality show' on which upstanding people of the society could bet on. They were gambling on which one of you would bite the dust first. I made them believe that the activities in the house were supposedly to push you all to do the 'right' thing and win them some sweet dough and also giving them some perverse ecstasy at the agony of others. It was like having ortolan bunting, except that people were watching here and they did not cover their faces but hid themselves in the bowels of the internet. I routed some of the investments which were made on all of you. These investments funded the logistics and operations and also, most importantly, your future."

"So, you stole from the despicable and notorious people who hide in the bowels of the Deep Web while emotionally manipulating five vulnerable people with their turbulent lives to bare themselves for the satisfaction of debauchery seeking delinquents."

"Well, that's the gist of it, if you chose to forget the intention."

"And indulge me, what might that be?

"For the greater good."

"For the greater good," repeated Rajesh with a smirk as he caressed his forehead with a slight shake of his head.

"Do not worry Rajesh. I understand your concern and consternation. You are all safe, relatively speaking."

"Relatively speaking. How convenient."

"No… that's the thing. The number on the folder which I had given to you at the start of this experiment. I would have written to you with clear instructions if you had not visited. Any number to word convertor gives you the location for you to find the locker. The second number is for you to open the locker. It is ready for you all. The portal. The experiment only ends and with success if all of you use it. It is your wardrobe, your gateway to Narnia. It is up to you Rajesh. You are the figure of authority. Convince them. There are new identities for The Famous Five. Gosh… that would be a blast… Enid Blyton on LSD…," said Yazdaan with a grin, "The skimmed cream is enough to at least start a new life. I have used most to prepare and organize this. I have also transferred some amount to all the NGOs that all of you visited. The rest is all yours. It is not much but it is enough to see the sunrise. There are new identities with new passports. A new beginning, a new birth, a new life. Please Rajesh, do not let the trial go in vain. It would just be a diabolical puppet show if the locker is not used to nourish your lives."

"And what about you Yazdaan?"

"As insurance, I had to give a validated ID, albeit a false one, which, in time, will lead them to me. I refused to change my name even when we were struggling with the haunting of the ghosts after my father's deeds. But I changed it now to safeguard you. To safeguard my subjects."

"You were Dr. Aman Abbas for us too."

"Yes. Aman. Peace. The most cherished thing that my father hoped after his accident. Oh well…. Coming back, the data analyzers are opportunists and have no clue about me. There is a core group of seven who controlled everything, the moderators and admins, called The Abyss. I was their single point of contact. Their local contractors might be my guest anytime now. I will close the loop with them. But rest assured, the subjects are safe. And their future too, if you comply."

"It is all too much to take in," said Rajesh after a long and brooding moment. Psychiatrists are primed to always be objective in their approach. Not to diagnose with either their own or the subject's emotion prying on their conscience, but this was stretching it to the extreme. But he knew that he would use the locker. Fourteen years spent behind bars and the regular talks with Yazdaan had pushed him into the experiment. All of them had paid their debts to the society, they had been through and out the justice system. The 'research' and the interactions with the other four had reignited the spark of life again in not just him but all of them. But it was just a spark. The locker was the fuel to keep it burning. Yes, he knew they would use the locker. The experiment was not in vain. They were not manipulated for nothing. It was indeed a success.

"I would love to discuss this further, but I am terribly sorry for being a bad host, but we must wrap this up. Things to do, people to host and such," said Yazdaan looking at his watch kept on the table.

"Are you telling me what I think you are?"

"It's goodbye Rajesh. This is my redemption."

It was well over an hour since Rajesh had left. He had insisted that Rajesh leave right in the middle of the downpour. But he was contented. As the rain died down, there was a tremendous calm which settled over him. He took the small wrist watch and caressed it and looked at the dial. It was well past three in the morning. He opened the small cabinet under his desk and took the compact Ruger LCR revolver out and released the safety lock. He kept it on the table and switched off the small table lamp and tied the watch to his left hand. He could feel the sudden surge of warmth. It was as if he was in the arms of his father, the slow tick of the watch was like the comforting beat of abu's heart. With a contented smile on his face, he closed his eyes. He was back in the valley and the ever-elusive spring time was in full swing. The sun shined without inhibition and the mountains wore a crown of flowers around their white head. He could smell his ammi preparing the wazwan feast only for him. It was his birthday. A time to celebrate. "Aman," said Yazdaan.

* * *